Drake

TWILIGHT FALLS BOOK FIVE

A.M. SALINGER

COPYRIGHT

Drake (Twilight Falls #5)
Copyright © 2021 by A.M. Salinger
All rights reserved. Registered with the US Copyright Office.
Second paperback edition: 2024
ISBN: 978-1-9162270-3-3

www.AMSalinger.com
shop.adstarrling.com

Edited by www.ElfwerksEditing.com
Cover Design by A.M. Salinger

BOOKS BY A.M. SALINGER

Nights

One Night - 1

The Escort - 2

Tokyo Heat - 3

Sweet Obsession - 4

Sweet Possession - 5

The Proposition - 6

Undisclosed - 7

Hush - 8

One Day - 9

Twilight Falls

Alex - 1

Carter - 2

Hunter - 3

Wyatt - 4

Drake - 5

Tristan - 6

Miles - 7

CONTENT NOTE

Drake (Twilight Falls #5) contains references to domestic violence, child neglect, and child physical abuse rooted in one of the characters' past. It is mentioned during a conversation between the two main characters. There is one scene where one of the characters is physically threatened as an adult in the current timeline.

CHAPTER ONE

Roman Campbell took a sip of his sparkling water and observed the two men taking to the floor for their first dance as a married couple.

Carter Wilson and Elijah Davis looked blissfully happy as they swayed to a classic Sinatra song, fingers interlocked and arms around one another while their bodies brushed sensuously. It was clear to everyone in the marquee that the grooms only had eyes for each other.

A twinge of jealousy stabbed through Roman at the happiness radiating on the two men's faces. Carter laughed at something Elijah said and took his husband's mouth in a hot kiss that had their guests clapping and wolf-whistling.

The newlyweds turned and extended their hands toward a pretty little blond girl in a cream taffeta and lace dress who stood watching them from the sidelines. Maisie, Carter's niece and his and Elijah's newly adopted daughter, squealed and ran out to join them. The couple caught her into their arms and resumed their dance, their mouths split in beaming smiles.

Roman swallowed a grimace.

I really am an asshole. I should be happy for them.

He'd been somewhat surprised to receive an invite to what was being touted as the most exclusive celebrity wedding of the year. Though he was friends with Carter, they hadn't spoken for a while, their busy lives meaning their paths rarely crossed except at social events.

They'd met five years ago, at an exclusive sex club in L.A. It was the kind of place where the world-famous clientele could indulge in their private desires and fantasies to their heart's content, without fear of their secrets becoming fodder for the paparazzi.

It had been Roman's first time at the club. He'd hit on Carter the minute he'd walked inside the place, not realizing that the tall man with the dirty blond hair and the body to die for was *the* A-list Hollywood actor who had practically dominated entertainment news ever since he exploded on the movie scene with his first blockbuster.

Though Carter had flirted with Roman, he hadn't obliged his invitation to visit one of the club's private suites for some down and dirty time. He had, however, kept a close eye on him.

Roman had been more than a little drunk and high on drugs when he'd made the impulsive decision to visit the club that night and hook up with a stranger, a fact he had been lambasted for at length when his manager and best friend James Lang turned up and dragged him from the place a couple of hours later.

"At least you had the decency to pick somewhere the paparazzi couldn't find you!" James had snapped the next morning while Roman lay recovering from his monumental hangover on the sundeck of his L.A. penthouse. "It's a good thing Carter messaged me when he did."

"Carter?" Roman had frowned at the unfamiliar name. "Who the hell is Carter? And could you pipe down? This headache is killing me," he'd added on a groan.

James had clenched and unclenched his hands in a way that told Roman he'd wished they were wrapped around Roman's neck.

"Carter is the guy you were hitting on last night," James had explained icily. "He's a friend of mine." He'd paused and narrowed his eyes at Roman, a muscle dancing in his cheek. "That headache isn't the only thing that's gonna kill you, Roman. You need to cut back on the booze and the drugs. You're not just ruining your health. You're sabotaging your career!"

The guilt and anger that had rotted Roman's insides for as long as he could remember flared into life and had his mouth curving in a nasty smile.

"Are you saying that as my best friend or as my manager?"

The hurt in James's eyes had Roman immediately regretting his harsh words.

"I'm sorry," Roman had mumbled in the stiff silence. "I promise I won't do anything like this again."

James had watched him for a moment before blowing out a heavy sigh. They'd both known it was a lie.

It wouldn't be another two years until Roman finally kept his word. By then, the whole of L.A. and the world knew that the lead singer of Crazyknot was damaged goods.

Paradoxically, Roman's soul-crushing fall from grace only boosted sales of their albums and propelled the band to international stardom. It also turned him into an overnight icon, one he'd assumed the entertainment industry would soon forget. Which made his and Crazyknot's shockingly successful comeback twelve months ago all the more humbling. Apparently, the world loved nothing more than seeing a former bad boy reform.

Roman's lips tilted in a self-deprecating smile. *Well, almost reform.*

He might have ditched the alcohol and the drugs. It didn't mean he'd turned into a monk. He scanned the marquee, the restless feeling that had been gnawing at his insides a sure-fire sign that he needed to let off some steam in a way that didn't involve getting intoxicated.

Now, let's find a guy I can have some fun with.

"I know that look," someone said next to him.

Roman closed his eyes briefly. He twisted on the bar stool and studied the man who'd taken the seat beside him with a faint frown.

James Lang looked his usual cool and elegant self in

a bottle green tuxedo that matched his eyes and framed specs.

Roman pursed his lips.

If it wasn't for the fact that he'd known James for thirteen years and had seen him puke his guts up on more occasions than he could count when they were teenagers, he might have taken a stab at the guy. James was attractive in the kind of way that made people pause and wonder what lay beneath the impeccable suits and hard exterior.

The only ones who truly knew the infamous manager were the members of Crazyknot and their close friends. For behind the cool, controlled facade James projected burned a fiery and surprisingly passionate soul.

To this day, Roman didn't know what had turned the outgoing and fun-loving boy he had come to know during what had been the most challenging years of his teenage life, into the stern and reserved man who now sat facing him. It had happened shortly after their first national tour.

Roman and the other members of Crazyknot had long questioned James about his almost overnight transformation, but the manager had always remained tight-lipped on the subject.

"Oh yeah?" Roman grumbled presently. "And what kind of look am I wearing, pray tell?"

James arched an eyebrow. He took a sip of his champagne before leaning in closer. "The kind that says you're looking for a good fuck."

Choked off laughter erupted close by.

James stiffened and looked over Roman's head.

Roman turned, a frown on his face and his mouth parting on a biting remark.

His breath locked in his throat.

Gunmetal blue eyes sparkled with mirth opposite him. Though the stranger straddled the bar stool in a relaxed pose, Roman could tell he was tall and would tower over him by a good few inches. His overlong, sun-kissed brown hair teased the collar of his classic, black tuxedo, the suit doing little to hide the hard angles and solid muscles beneath the expensive material. Silver peppered his short beard and sideburns, framing a rugged, tanned face that wouldn't look out of place on the cover of an outdoor sports magazine. His fingers were hard and callused where he held a half-empty beer bottle.

The man smiled and tipped his drink at them with a nonchalant dip of his head. "Don't mind me. I'm just here for the beer."

Roman's cock stirred. He swallowed.

Fuck.

Mr. Sideburns was one hundred percent his type. And he looked exactly like the kind of trouble Roman needed to avoid tonight.

CHAPTER TWO

DRAKE JACKSON WATCHED THE MAN WITH THE MOCHA eyes stiffen.

He'd clocked the guy an hour ago, just before the wedding ceremony. From the buzz that had danced through the crowd when the stranger had walked into the enchanting woodland clearing where Carter and Elijah had decided to get married, it seemed he was an A-list celebrity of sorts.

Though his face was vaguely familiar, Drake hadn't been able to put a name to it. He wasn't someone who made it a life goal of keeping up with entertainment news. There was, however, no denying that the stranger was drop dead gorgeous.

The wine-red tuxedo the guy wore hinted at a lean, toned build and his flawless, cream rose boutonnière contrasted prettily with his honey-colored skin. Silver studs decorated his earlobes, highlighting the beautiful Phoenix tattoo rising up the left side of his neck.

The man was alluring in the kind of way that

brought to mind satin sheets and a dark room that smelled of sex.

Hot Guy twisted his full lips in an irritated moue. "Do you make it a habit of eavesdropping?"

Drake's gaze lingered on his mouth.

"No," he drawled, amused. "I gotta admit though, I am intrigued by your conversation." He looked over Hot Guy's shoulder to the Guard Dog who'd been scowling at him for the last fifteen seconds and decided to tease the two men. "Are you looking for a threesome?"

The Guard Dog's expression went from annoyed to disgusted in a heartbeat. "Hell no! And FYI, we are *not* a couple." He cocked a disparaging thumb at Hot Guy.

It was Hot Guy's turn to scowl. "Hey! You think you're too good for me, asshole?!"

The Guard Dog arched an eyebrow. "I *know* I'm too good for you, kid. Besides, your tastes in the bedroom leave something to be desired."

Drake's curiosity deepened. It was clear the two men were close friends. It was also apparent the Guard Dog was used to keeping Hot Guy on some kind of leash.

"Just because you like to do it missionary style doesn't mean my sexual preferences are indecent," Hot Guy snapped. "And you're only six months older than me."

Guard Dog rolled his eyes at that. "How do you know the grooms?" he asked Drake gruffly.

"I'm one of Carter's childhood friends."

Hot Guy straightened on his stool. "Oh. You're from around here?"

Drake downed the rest of his beer and smiled laconically. "Yup. Born and raised."

It was all he was willing to say on the subject. The folks of Twilight Falls knew of his sordid family background. He saw no reason to inform a couple of perfect strangers about it too.

"Ah." Understanding dawned on the Guard Dog's face. "Are you one of those Terrible Seven I've heard so much about?"

Interest sparked in Hot Guy's eyes. "Oh yeah. Carter mentioned something about that a few times, didn't he?" He arched an eyebrow at Drake. "So, you and Carter were in some kind of gang?"

"If you call spray painting the principal's car a racy red when we were in middle school gang-like behavior, then, yes."

The Guard Dog smiled. "I'm James. James Lang. I'm an old friend of Carter's from L.A." He offered his hand to Drake.

Drake shook it. "Drake Jackson."

"You probably know who this troublesome guy is." James indicated Hot Guy.

"I don't, actually," Drake said steadily.

James blinked. He burst out laughing in the next instant, the sound drawing the stares of several of the guests.

Drake suppressed a smile.

Hot Guy looked conflicted, as if debating whether to be shocked or offended.

"Well, I'll leave you two to get to know one another." James patted Hot Guy's shoulder, a mocking grin pasted across his face. "Don't do anything I wouldn't do," he said on a parting shot as he headed into the crowd.

Hot Guy turned until he was facing the bar once more. He twisted his glass a couple of times before knocking back his drink. "You really don't know who I am?" He glanced sideways at Drake.

Drake dragged his gaze from Hot Guy's lips and throat.

Even the way the guy swallowed was sexy.

"No, I don't." Drake smiled faintly. "Does that hurt your ego?"

Surprise flashed in Hot Guy's eyes, turning his irises a dark caramel.

"No," he admitted quietly. "It's kinda refreshing, to be honest."

Drake waited. When it became clear the man was not going to offer his name, he waved the bartender over.

"Could I have another beer? And he'll have—" He raised an eyebrow.

"Sparkling water," Hot Guy murmured. "Thank you."

Drake studied him curiously. "You're not drinking?"

Hot Guy's face turned guarded. "No."

Drake suspected there was a story there.

The bartender brought their order over.

"Are you in town just for the wedding?" Drake asked lightly.

"Yeah. James and I are heading back to L.A. tonight."

Drake toyed with his beer bottle. "What your friend said earlier. Was it true?"

Hot Guy blinked, confused.

Drake deliberately lowered his gaze to the man's mouth. "Are you looking for a good fuck?"

Hot Guy's lips parted on a sharp inhale.

Drake looked up and saw desire darken the man's eyes. His own pulse quickened.

He wasn't sure what had gotten into him. He wasn't the kind of guy to hook up with a stranger. Although he'd had his fair share of one-night stands in the past, these days he preferred short affairs that ended by mutual agreement. He wasn't made for long term relationships, something he made clear to anyone he intended to sleep with.

Maybe it's because of the wedding.

Seeing Career and Elijah get married so soon after Alex Hancock tied the knot with Finn West only reminded Drake of the painful fact that he was the one member of the Terrible Seven destined to remain single. It didn't help that Alex was the person he thought he might have committed to being in a relationship with one day. Except Drake had been too much of a coward to admit this to him. By the time he realized how much Alex meant to him, his friend had left Twilight Falls for San Diego.

Although seeing Alex with Finn had hurt at first after the lawyer returned to town, Drake was glad that his former lover had found someone he wanted to spend the rest of his life with. Alex deserved to be happy, as did Finn.

"What are you saying?" Hot Guy said hoarsely.

Drake decided honesty was the best course of action. "I have zero interest in starting something serious. If you're in the mood to have some fun, I'd be happy to oblige."

Hot Guy's pupils flared. His gaze burned Drake's skin.

"Are you sure you can satisfy me?"

Drake's cock roused at the open challenge on the other man's face.

"Why don't we go somewhere private and find out?"

CHAPTER THREE

SHIT.

Roman's heart thudded wildly against his ribs at the open invitation in Drake's eyes. It had been a long time since he'd been this aroused. And the guy who'd brought him to such a fever pitch state hadn't even touched him yet.

His brain knew this was a terrible idea. His mouth thought otherwise.

"Okay," Roman mumbled.

Drake's smile raised goosebumps on his skin. Roman climbed off the bar stool and followed Drake as the man headed leisurely for the exit. To his surprise, Drake crossed the grounds and made his way toward the forest that surrounded the modern, wood and glass mansion overlooking the creek at the bottom of a shallow valley.

It wasn't until they were in the shadows of the tree line that Drake took Roman's hand.

"Be careful. The ground is uneven around here."

Roman nodded mutely. Drake's touch scorched his skin and was doing all kinds of strange things to his breathing.

"I gotta admit, I've never made out in the woods before," he muttered as Drake led him deeper into the trees.

Drake flashed a grin at him, white teeth glinting in the gloom.

"You haven't?" he teased.

Roman frowned. "No. Unlike you, I like the comfort of a bed."

"And satin sheets, no doubt."

Roman stared. "What?"

"Nothing."

"It was something," Roman blurted.

"Are you always this stubborn?"

"Yes."

Drake chuckled. "There's no need to sound so proud about it. And if you want the truth, the first thing I thought of when I saw you was satin sheets and a dark bedroom."

Roman narrowed his eyes suspiciously. "What? And that's it?"

Drake tugged Roman through a thicket and pushed him against a tree shielded by greenery. Roman gasped when Drake dipped his head and nipped at his chin with his teeth.

"No," Drake said hotly inches from Roman's lips. "I also imagined you naked on the bed, your cock spent and your body covered in cum."

Oh God.

Roman finally gave in to the insane desire bubbling through his veins and grasped Drake's face. Their mouths met in a hard kiss.

Drake explored the shape of Roman's lips before pushing past them, his movements commanding as he sucked and licked and tugged on Roman's trembling tongue. Roman moaned, his legs growing weak with pleasure and his dick pressing painfully against the zipper of his trousers.

Drake made a low sound and spread Roman's thighs with a powerful knee. Roman groaned when Drake massaged his erection with his leg.

Drake traced Roman's throat with his fingers, his touch lingering on his tattoo for a moment before dancing down his chest. He paused over the shape of the beaded ring piercing Roman's left nipple and gave it a playful tug.

"*Fuck!*" Roman hissed, hips bucking.

"I'm afraid I'm going to have to draw the line at actually fucking you." Drake nudged Roman's chin up and pressed hungry kisses to his neck, his beard grazing Roman's sensitive skin in a way he didn't dislike. "But I *am* going to pleasure you until you scream."

Drake went down on his knees, unbuckled Roman's belt, and tugged his pants and boxers low on his hips.

Roman's belly contracted when the cool night air kissed his naked, weeping erection. Then there was heat and wetness and the scorching depths of Drake's mouth.

Roman gasped and panted as Drake swallowed his

cock in languorous motions, his clever tongue wrapping skillfully around Roman's turgid flesh.

Drake fixed Roman's hips with his hands and started blowing him slow and deep, his breaths washing in and out of his nose while he took Roman all the way to the back of his throat over and over again.

Blood thundered in Roman's ears. He bowed his body, his fingers finding Drake's hair in a punishing grip and his mouth opening on wanton moans. Pleasure swamped him with every sinful movement of Drake's mouth on his aching cock. It wasn't long before Roman felt his orgasm tickle his toes and balls.

Surprise jolted him when Drake let go of his erection and pushed his pants all the way down to his ankles. Drake freed Roman's left leg and hooked it over his shoulder, opening him up.

"What are you—?" Roman mumbled.

He stiffened when he heard foil rustle and rip in the gloom. Drake's eyes gleamed beneath him as he took Roman's cock inside his mouth once more.

Roman bit his lip and dropped his head back against the tree, the delicious heat of his climax surging through him all over again. He froze when he felt Drake's fingers dip beneath his aching balls and stroke his trembling taint.

"*Ahhh!*"

Roman's shocked cry turned into a hiss when Drake probed his hole with two lube-slicked, condom-covered fingers. Drake let go of Roman's dick.

"How long has it been since you've had a man inside you?" he growled, circling the swollen, sensitive head of Roman's erection with his tongue at the same time he rubbed the tight folds of Roman's opening.

"Too long!" Roman gasped, hips jerking.

Drake stilled for a moment. Roman looked down and met his heated stare.

"Is that true?"

"Yes," Roman whispered. "I haven't had a—*Oh God!*"

Roman brought his knuckles to his mouth and bit down hard to muffle his cry of pleasure as Drake slipped his thick fingers inside him. His passage burned and stung, the ring of muscles guarding his entrance contracting against the sudden penetration.

Though he felt naked and vulnerable where he stood half-naked and braced against the tree, Roman somehow knew Drake would guide him to the other side of this intoxicating sexual encounter safely.

"Do you like it soft and slow?" Drake moved his fingers slickly in and out of Roman's hole, stretching him wider each time. "Or do you prefer it hard and fast?"

Roman keened as Drake started fucking him with deep, strong thrusts. While light exploded in front of his eyes when Drake's probing fingertips found the soft bump of his prostate.

"Oh yes!" Roman groaned. "*Like that!* Jesus fuck, that feels good!"

An animal sound left Drake. He kept up the punishing pace and took Roman's dripping cock inside his mouth once more, his stubble scratching Roman's thighs and balls as he blew him hard and deep.

Roman's orgasm soon raced down his spine and

stiffened his back. A buzzing sound filled his head. He came on a hoarse shout, his entire body convulsing with spasms of ecstasy. His hips powered his pulsing cock forcefully in and out of Drake's lips and his hole contracted hungrily on Drake's fingers as he filled Drake's mouth with hot cum.

It felt like ages before Roman came to his senses. Drake had pulled out of his body and was on his feet once more. Roman shivered when he felt Drake's lips on his throat. Drake's breaths were hot and heavy against his flesh.

Roman looked down dazedly.

Drake had freed his own erection and was rubbing himself briskly.

Roman's eyes widened and his ass tightened reflexively when he saw Drake's thick, veiny cock. He licked his lips and dropped a hand to Drake's throbbing flesh.

"Let me," Roman breathed.

Drake faltered before nodding. He fisted his hands on the tree trunk on either side of Roman's head and leaned down to take Roman's mouth in a searing kiss.

Roman stilled and moaned when he tasted himself on Drake's tongue. Drake punched his hips demandingly. Roman complied to Drake's silent command and started stroking his meaty cock, fingers eagerly exploring the silken skin and corded veins covering Drake's shaft.

Drake's lusty groans filled Roman's ears as he thrust his erection harder and faster through Roman's fingers.

Roman's toes curled, an echo of his orgasm dancing through his back passage.

He wanted nothing more than to have Drake's dick inside his body right now.

Drake's breathing hitched a moment later. He grabbed a handkerchief from inside his tuxedo and covered his cock and Roman's hand as he came with powerful jerking motions, his breaths mingling with Roman's where they still kissed.

A noise reached Roman dimly through the blood pounding in his ears.

Light washed over them.

Someone murmured a hasty, "Oh. I'm sorry!" before disappearing in the night.

Roman stiffened in alarm.

"Sshhh," Drake whispered against Roman's mouth. "He didn't see you."

Roman's heart slammed painfully against his ribs. Memories of the last scandal that had rocked his life and brought his world crashing down around him blasted through his mind, cooling his lust as effectively as a bucket of cold water.

This was a mistake!

"I—I'm sorry!" Roman mumbled. "I have to go!" He avoided Drake's eyes, pulled his trousers up, and hastily straightened his clothes before dashing off into the darkness.

CHAPTER FOUR

Drake stared. "You're kidding me?"

"I'm not," Hunter Thomson replied. "My realtor friend told me about it yesterday."

Drake glared into his coffee. It was late morning and they were having breakfast at *La Petite Bouche Gourmande*, Elijah's popular bakery and eatery. Although the place was packed, Elijah had gotten into the habit of reserving a table for Carter and the rest of the Terrible Seven near the back.

"Damn." Drake frowned. "I had enough saved up to put an offer on the place this month."

Hunter grimaced sympathetically. "I'd love to say you'll find somewhere else, but that house really was one of a kind."

Drake sat back in his chair and raked his hair with a hand, frustration bringing a bitter taste in his mouth.

The Strickland Estate had long held a special place in his heart. The property of an eccentric millionaire who'd made Twilight Falls his home in the 1940s, the rambling, two-story Colonial Revival mansion with its tennis court, swimming pool, and guest house occupied ten acres of prime woodland on the northern edge of Twilight Falls.

He'd stumbled across it by accident some fifteen years ago, when he was roaming the forest behind his neighborhood to get away from his squabbling parents and the rundown, clapboard house he called his home. Although the mansion had long since fallen into a state of disrepair, Drake had fallen in love with it at first sight. He'd visited it many a times since and had promised himself he would buy it one day and restore it to its former glory.

It was a vow he thought he would soon be able to fulfill. His building business had come in leaps and bounds in the last decade and he was about to turn a seven-figure profit for the second consecutive year thanks to a big renovation contract that was about to land in his lap.

That someone had purchased the property he had long coveted right from under his nose irked him almost as badly as the restless feeling that had been bubbling under his skin for the last two months. A restless feeling that had everything to do with a certain man with mocha-colored eyes and a face and body he couldn't forget.

Drake had since found out who his mystery man from Carter's wedding was. And it was immediately clear to him that the guy was *way* out of his league.

"Any idea who bought the place?" Drake said

gruffly, pushing the distracting images of Roman Campbell's caramel skin and full lips to the back of his mind.

Hunter shook his head. "My friend wouldn't say. I get the feeling he signed an NDA. All he hinted at was that it was some rich guy from L.A."

Drake clenched his jaw. Considering the price tag on the place, a non-disclosure agreement meant that whoever bought the Strickland Estate was probably some kind of celebrity. The town of Twilight Falls had become increasingly popular with the wealthy crowd in L.A. in the last few years and even more so after the world found out it was the home of Carter Wilson and Finn West. Add to this the town's ideal location in the San Bernardino Mountains and its popularity as a holiday destination for thrill seekers and those seeking a slower pace of life alike, and Drake could understand why the property market in Twilight Falls was booming.

It was a fact the local mayor and town council were all too keenly aware of. Much to the townsfolk's relief, the council had instituted rules that meant outsiders had to fulfill several strict criteria to be able to purchase homes and land in and around the famous town. No one wanted to see the people who'd been born here driven out of the place by rocketing property prices.

"There you are," someone called out behind Drake.

Drake turned around. A smartly dressed guy with dark hair and hazel eyes was making his way toward their table. Hunter's mouth split in a beaming smile.

Theo Miller greeted Drake, slipped into the chair next to Hunter, and leaned across to kiss his lover, heedless of the admiring stares he was drawing. "Imogen didn't know where you were."

Hunter slid his fingers through Theo's where he'd laid his hand on the table.

Imogen Hart was the manager of *Go Thomson!*, Hunter's sports and apparel shop and one of the most successful retail businesses this side of the San Bernardino Mountains. The fact that Hunter's direct competitor was Theo's own place across the road from *Go Thomson!* hadn't gotten in the way of the two men's burgeoning relationship. They'd even moved in together a few weeks ago, Theo finally abandoning the rental place he'd been occupying since he relocated to Twilight Falls to open the latest branch of his successful clothing chain.

A young woman with pink and blue pixie hair came over with a cup of coffee for Theo and topped off their drinks.

"I see you two love birds are still in the honeymoon phase of your relationship," Sam Harris said acerbically as she eyed Hunter and Theo's entwined fingers.

Hunter grinned. "Is that jealousy I detect in your voice?"

"Yeah, well, some of us aren't getting any," Elijah's bakery manager grumbled.

"*The Watering Hole* has a new bartender." Hunter wriggled his eyebrows. "I reckon she might be your type."

Sam perked up. "Really?"

"She's pretty nice," Theo concurred. "And she makes a mean margarita."

Sam smiled. "Looks like I might have to ask Elijah to let me leave early tomorrow night." She caught Drake's expression. "What's wrong with him?"

"Someone bought the house he'd had his eye on for a while," Hunter said. "You know the Strickland Estate?"

Sam raised an eyebrow. "The abandoned place outside of town? The one's that's supposed to be haunted?"

"There's a haunted house in Twilight Falls?" Theo said uneasily.

"No, there isn't," Drake muttered. "The mansion is just old and dilapidated."

A devilish light shone in Hunter's eyes as he observed his lover. "Are you scared of haunted houses?"

"No, I'm not," Theo denied quickly.

Hunter grinned mischievously.

"Boy, are you in trouble," Sam told Theo in a commiserating tone. "This guy here is the prankster of the Terrible Seven."

"Don't worry," Theo said. "I have my ways of handling him."

Hunter stared. "Oh yeah? And how are you intending to *handle* me, exactly?"

"I'll withhold sex for a week if you try anything stupid," Theo stated firmly.

Hunter's face fell. "You wouldn't!"

"Oh, believe me, I would." Theo raised an eyebrow.

"After all, everyone in town knows you can't resist—" he indicated his own body with a hand, "—*this*."

"Wow. I hadn't realized your ego had overgrown the size of your dick." Hunter scowled. "Well, we'll see about that, Hot Shot."

"Ten dollars says he doesn't last four days," Sam told Drake.

"Make it twenty bucks and a day," Drake drawled.

Theo chuckled while his lover spluttered.

Drake's mouth curved in a smile, thoughts of the Strickland Estate fading from his mind for a moment. His cell phone rang. He fished it out of his jeans, saw the number, and took the call.

"Hi, Lara."

Lara Sheppard's voice was full of restrained excitement. "Hey, Drake. Can you talk?"

"Yeah. Give me a second." Drake rose and walked over to a quiet part of the bakery. "What's up?"

Lara was one of the local area's up and coming architects. Born and bred in Twilight Falls, she'd relocated to the town two years ago with her husband and her two children, leaving a high-flying career in Philadelphia to open up her own firm. Drake had collaborated with her on a few projects in and around Twilight Falls and found her easy to work with. They were both driven and sticklers for perfection, a fact that had earned them a coveted reputation in the San Bernardino Mountains.

"I can finally tell you about the secret project I wanted to hire you for. The client closed on the property yesterday."

Drake stilled. "Yesterday?"

Unease coiled through him.

No. It can't be. That would be a sick twist of fate.

"Yeah. It's the Strickland Estate."

Drake's stomach plummeted to his boots.

"And you're not going to believe who the client is," Lara gushed. "It's Roman Campbell."

CHAPTER FIVE

"It's official," James said leadenly. "You've lost your fucking mind."

Roman chuckled, switched off the engine of the RV, and climbed out of the vehicle. James followed reluctantly.

They walked up the graveled drive, stopped at the bottom of a flight of shallow stone steps, and stared at the run-down mansion straddling the rise above them.

Ivy and wisteria covered the wide, columned porch and pale facade of the sprawling, Colonial mansion. A section of the hipped roof had collapsed, along with a dormer and part of the brick chimney that had once graced the west wing. The once pretty leaded windows were covered in grime and the entrance door with its colored glass sidelights was ajar, the rotting wood having expanded over time and made it difficult to shut.

"I can't believe you bought this place without letting

me know about it," James grumbled. "I'm your manager, for Christ's sake!"

"You're the one who kept saying I should invest some of my considerable fortune in property." Roman gazed steadily at James. "Look, I know you're still worried about me and will likely do so for the rest of your life. But it's been eighteen months since I came out of rehab. I'm clean and I intend to stay that way."

James hesitated before raking his hair with a hand. "I know. I know I should trust you. And I do. I want you to know that. But—," he paused, a guilty light flashing in his eyes for a moment, "I don't want to see you and the band suffer through that hell again."

Guilt twisted Roman's stomach at the pained look in James's eyes. Roman knew more than anyone else how badly the ghosts of his past had come to bite not just him, but the friends who had carried him through the darkest years of his life in the ass three years ago, on the day his world fell apart for the second time.

Nearly half a decade after Crazyknot emerged on the rock 'n' roll scene and shot to international stardom, its lead singer had gotten high on cocaine and alcohol and thrashed a function room at one of the most lauded celebrity gatherings in Hollywood. The scandal had dominated the entertainment news channels for days and even made national headlines, the picture of an intoxicated and wild-eyed Roman being hustled into the back of a car by his friends and manager forever branding him an unstable troublemaker.

The only ones who'd known the real reason why

he'd fallen apart that day were James and the other four members of Crazyknot. Even though they'd supported him over the volatile years of his addiction, Roman had known from their expressions when he'd woken up in a hotel the next morning drenched in sweat that that incident had been the final straw.

It was James who'd told him the reason they'd stayed in the room that night and taken turns to watch over him was because Roman had tried to kill himself several times. And it was James who'd resisted the others' arguments that Roman be confined to a psychiatric hospital for his own good.

Instead, his best friend had booked a private jet to take Roman to an exclusive rehabilitation resort in the Nevada Desert. And he'd stayed with Roman those first few crucial weeks while Roman had gone into acute withdrawal.

Roman was all too aware that the reason he was still alive today was because of the men who had stood by him since he was sixteen, especially James. Just as he knew that if he let them coddle him for the rest of his life, he would never move on from his dark past and heal fully.

"Why this place?" James waved a hand vaguely at the overgrown estate. "Why not somewhere closer, in L.A.?"

"Because I like it here. It's pretty and it's remote." Roman shrugged. "I can still commute to the studio. And I'm keeping my penthouse for when I need to stay in L.A."

James frowned. "You've only been to Twilight Falls

once. How the hell can you be so sure you're gonna like it here?"

Roman grinned and patted him on the shoulder. "That's where you're wrong, my friend. Now, how about I show you around the place?"

Roman had just finished his impromptu tour of the property and its dilapidated outbuildings when the sound of an engine rose from the front of the mansion. He and James circumnavigated the empty pool and the side of the house in time to see a canary yellow Audi appear around the bend in the winding driveway.

The brightly colored car pulled up behind James's silver Jaguar where they'd towed it at the back of Roman's rental RV. A tall blonde with sun glasses and a laptop climbed out of the Audi as the two men started down the overgrown, terraced lawn.

"Wow." The woman pushed her glasses up on her head and studied the mansion with a pensive look as they headed toward her. "I'd forgotten how crazy pretty this place was."

James eyed her as if she'd lost her mind.

She laughed and extended a hand. "Hi, I'm Lara Sheppard, Roman's architect for this project. You must be James."

James reluctantly shook her hand. "How did you know who I was?"

Lara smiled. "Because Roman said he was bringing his handsome but grumpy best friend with him today." She ignored the dark look James cast at Roman, rooted around the pocket of her coat, and fished out a set of keys. "Here." She dropped them in Roman's hand. "You are now the official owner of the Strickland Estate."

A quiet feeling of satisfaction blossomed inside Roman as he curled his fingers around the cool metal. Although he'd owned the penthouse in L.A. for several years, he'd never truly considered it his home. The place was too modern and soulless for his liking, like the rest of the city.

"How exactly did you find this place?" James asked Roman curiously. "And how often have you actually been here?"

"I saw the 'For Sale' sign when we came for Carter's wedding," Roman said as they strolled up the steps to the porch. "I was intrigued enough by the setting to look into it further."

"Roman got in touch with me via the realtor six weeks ago," Lara added. "He's viewed the property some dozen times since, while his offer was being processed and surveys were being carried out. It's the reason why we'll be able to begin reconstruction straightaway. We started drawing up plans a while back."

"When do we get started?" Roman said as they entered the house, unable to hide the thrill in his voice.

He'd only ever felt this way when he was in the studio recording a new song. For some reason he couldn't explain, he'd fallen in love with Twilight Falls when he'd first come here two months ago. The town with its surrounding forests and mountains instilled in him a sense of peace he hadn't felt in years.

The fact that the man he hadn't been able to get out of his mind for the past eight weeks lived there was a mere coincidence and hadn't factored in his decision to buy the estate.

Although, truth be told, I wouldn't actually mind seeing him again. Just to find out if what I felt that night was a fluke.

Roman's belly clenched as he thought of Drake. It had been forever since he'd experienced such mind-numbing pleasure in the arms of a man. He'd lost track of the number of times he'd jacked off to Drake's face since that unforgettable night in the forest.

Lara turned in the wide, marble hallway, her expression growing stilted. "About that. The builder I'd provisionally booked for the renovation pulled out at the last minute. It's gonna take a couple of weeks to find someone else."

Roman stopped and narrowed his eyes. "Pulled out? What do you mean? This is gonna be a pretty lucrative project for whoever takes it on. And didn't you say he was the best guy for the job this side of the San Bernardino Mountains?"

Lara grimaced. "I did. And he undoubtedly is."

"Then what the hell is his problem?" Roman said stiffly.

James frowned. "Isn't it a breach of contract if he withdraws his services so late in the game?"

Lara sighed. "We haven't actually signed anything yet, so no. And I wouldn't mess with the guy. Drake Jackson is an incredibly well-respected member of the Twilight Falls' community."

"Oh." James startled and glanced at Roman, surprised.

Roman's pulse quickened as he stared at Lara. "Did you say…Drake Jackson?!"

CHAPTER SIX

"Roman bought the Strickland Estate?" Carter's eyebrows rose so high they almost disappeared under his hairline.

"Keep your voice down." Drake glanced around the busy bar. "I don't think the guy wants the whole of Twilight Falls to find out yet."

Finn West took a sip of his drink. "Wow, I can't believe we're gonna have another celebrity in town."

"You kinda forget that you're a celebrity yourself, babe," Alex Hancock-West told his husband wryly. He directed a skeptical stare at Drake over his beer. "I gotta say, you're acting remarkably blasé about this development. I thought you were eyeing that place for yourself."

"You were?" Carter said, surprised.

Drake's fingers clenched around his whiskey glass. "There's not a lot I can do about it." He frowned. "The guy bought the place fair and square."

It had been a day since he'd learned that he'd lost

the house of his dreams to a man he thought he would never lay his eyes on again. A man he'd very much regretted not fucking that unforgettable night two months ago.

To say that he had mixed feelings about the whole thing would be understatement. The company of his friends and the buzz of alcohol were going some way to numb Drake's shock at the dual bombshell Lara had dropped on him yesterday.

He knew she'd been upset that he'd pulled out on the contract she'd proposed to him several weeks ago. Drake was aware the loss of income was something he shouldn't overlook lightly. But now that the goal he'd been working so hard to reach was no longer attainable, he couldn't see the point of taking on that particular job.

Besides, he didn't want to see Roman anytime soon. It would only twist the knife in an already raw wound.

"Still, I wonder why Roman decided to move here," Carter mused. "Twilight Falls is the last place I'd imagine someone like him living."

"You mean, because he's a world famous rockstar?" Alex frowned. "The flow of paparazzi had died down a bit since your wedding. I bet those leeches will be back in force once they find out the lead singer of Crazyknot intends to make the place his home too."

"The lead singer of Crazyknot is moving to Twilight Falls?" someone muttered in a surprised voice.

Tristan Hart joined them and took the seat next to Alex, his dark eyes full of curiosity.

Drake sighed. "Maybe we shouldn't have this conversation here."

"Have what conversation?" Hunter came up behind Tristan with Theo and a round of drinks. "What are we talking about?"

Carter glanced curiously toward the bar's entrance. "I thought Wyatt and Nathan were coming with you guys."

"They said they'd drop by later." Hunter grimaced. "I bet you they're fucking."

"Hunter," Theo groaned.

"What?" Hunter shrugged. "It's the truth."

Drake swallowed a sigh. Another member of the Terrible Seven who'd found his soulmate in the last month was Wyatt Batista, the owner of *Wolf Design*, a popular web and graphic firm in Twilight Falls.

Wyatt was the quietest member of the Terrible Seven and the one who'd always gotten into the least trouble among all of them. The fact that he'd been lusting after his business partner had come as a surprise to Drake. It hadn't taken him and the rest of the Terrible Seven long to realize Nathan was the ideal man for Wyatt, Nathan's extroverted personality a perfect match to Wyatt's reserved nature.

A group of women came through the front door in a rush of cool air. Although it wasn't that unusual for *The Watering Hole* to see a female clientele despite being the unofficial gay establishment for the area, the woman at the head of the trio stood out enough to make several of the men in the place pause and check her out.

"Well, there is *one* Batista in the house," Carter drawled.

Izzy Batista's stare landed on them with the accuracy of a heat-seeking missile. She made her way toward their table, Sam and Imogen in tow.

Izzy was Wyatt's younger sister and the unofficial eighth member of the Terrible Seven. She had been their advocate, tormentor, and troublesome matchmaker since middle school and still played a large role in all their lives.

Twilight Falls and the Terrible Seven wouldn't be the same without Izzy Batista and everyone knew it.

Izzy stopped at their table, propped her hands on Hunter and Theo's shoulders, and leaned forward conspiratorially.

"A little birdie told me Roman Campbell just bought a house in town!" she hissed in a low voice full of glee.

"What?!" Imogen gasped.

"Fuck me," Hunter mumbled.

"The rockstar? That Roman Campbell?!" Sam's shocked gaze swung to Drake. "Wait. Did he buy the—?"

"How the hell did you find out?" Drake scowled at Izzy.

Izzy waved a hand vaguely. "I have my sources." She narrowed her eyes at Sam. "You know which place he bought?"

Sam hesitated and glanced at Drake. "Well, the only notable property that sold in the last week is the old Strickland Estate."

Izzy's pressed a hand to her mouth, her round eyes

locked on Drake. "Isn't that place you had your eyes on?!"

"I did," Drake said stiffly. "Now, I would be grateful if everybody would shut up about it. In case you people didn't realize, I'm trying to drown my sorrows here."

"Poor baby." Izzy's expression cleared. "So, any of you guys seen him yet? I mean, that man is a serious hottie. I thought I was going to self-combust when I saw him at Carter and Elijah's wedding."

"His tattoo was something else," Sam murmured.

"And that red suit he wore was gorgeous," Imogen mumbled with a glazed expression.

The body beneath it was even more so.

Drake frowned at that errant thought.

"You ladies know Roman's gay, right?" Carter drawled.

"A woman can still fantasize," Izzy said haughtily. "Besides, we have two hot, single gay guys who can give him a run for his money right here." She indicated Tristan and Drake.

"You can count me out," Tristan murmured. "A rockstar would be way too much trouble."

Drake downed the rest of his whiskey.

Izzy arched an eyebrow. "You sure are being quiet."

Drake pointed at his empty glass. "Like I said, drowning my sorrows."

"I bet Roman would help you do that in a heartbeat," Izzy teased.

Drake maintained a neutral expression.

Izzy had the same ability to sniff out the truth as a bloodhound.

To Drake's dismay, the green eyes opposite him flared with suspicion. A commotion by the door distracted them.

Imogen gaped. "Er, isn't that—?"

CHAPTER SEVEN

THE NOISE OF THE BUSY CROWD FILLING *THE WATERING Hole* washed over Roman where he stood in the doorway of the bar. It subsided slightly in the next instant. He felt dozens of eyes on him as he dug his hands in the pockets of his denim jacket.

This is such *a stupid idea.*

Roman clenched his jaw. He'd come here with a single goal in mind and he was going to do it even if it killed him.

It was Lara who'd told him where he would likely find Drake tonight. Apparently, the man and his friends made it a habit to catch up with each other over a drink most Saturday nights.

"You're gonna try and change Drake's mind?" Lara had asked him doubtfully when he'd called her a few hours ago.

Roman couldn't blame the architect for her skepticism.

"Yes. If you say he's the best man for the job, then I don't want anyone else."

"I really don't think he'll agree to your proposition. Once he makes up his mind about something, nothing short of a miracle can make Drake alter his course of action."

Roman had smiled coldly at that. "I have nothing to lose by trying."

The gutsy statement he'd made to the architect echoed mockingly through his head. He brushed off the attention he was drawing and scanned the mostly male clientele packed inside the place.

It only took seconds to find Drake's table.

The place the Terrible Seven were seated at looked like an oasis in a storm. Roman headed determinedly across the room toward them, the crowd parting ahead of him like some kind of biblical sea.

"Hi, Roman," Carter said when Roman stopped at their table. "It's good to see you again."

"Hey, Carter." Roman acknowledged the movie star and his friends with a curt dip of his head. He ignored the avid curiosity on their faces and those of the three women who stood staring at him with stunned expressions, and directed a guarded stare at the man he'd come here to see.

Drake's eyes were dark blue pools filled with hostility as he looked at Roman over an empty glass.

Roman tried hard not to swallow.

He'd played this scenario over a dozen times in his head while he was riding his motorcycle into town.

Now that he was face to face with Drake, his carefully composed arguments flew straight out of his head.

In their stead came memories of that night. Of Drake's lips on his own. Of Drake's hot, wet mouth sucking his trembling cock. Of Drake's fingers plundering the most intimate part of his body and wringing a screaming orgasm from his throat.

"What do you want?"

Drake's cold words chilled Roman's libido and raised goosebumps on his skin. Roman gritted his teeth, conscious of the surprised glances Drake's friends were exchanging.

"Can we talk? In private."

For a moment, he thought Drake would refuse.

A muscle jumped in Drake's cheek. He pushed his chair back and rose to his feet. "Follow me."

Roman headed silently after him, aware of the hot stares drilling into their backs. Drake led him down a corridor and past some restrooms before walking out through a back door. They emerged on a terrace overlooking a private summer garden with a seating area.

Drake made for a shadowy corner of the porch and turned to face Roman. "Talk."

Irritation shot through Roman at Drake's curt tone, dampening his apprehension.

What the hell is his problem?!

Roman fisted his hands and raised his chin challengingly. "Why did you refuse the job?"

Drake arched an eyebrow. "Because I didn't want it."

Roman ignored his mocking comeback. "Lara said

you were on board until you found out I'd bought the place." He frowned. "Is that it? Is it because you'd be working for me?"

A strained silence fell between them.

Drake sighed, his shoulders sagging as if a weight had fallen off them.

"Yes and no," he murmured, his voice less gruff than it had been.

Roman folded his arms across his chest. "Elaborate."

Drake narrowed his eyes slightly at his bossy tone.

"The Strickland Estate was mine."

Surprise jolted Roman. "Come again?"

Drake rubbed the back of his neck, his expression growing awkward. "I've had my eye on that property for over a decade. You coming along and snatching it right from under my nose doesn't exactly make me happy."

Roman gaped, too shocked to speak for a moment.

"Wait. You wanted to buy that place? And now you're pissed because someone got to it before you?!" He threw his hands up in the air. "That's the dumbest thing I've ever heard!"

Drake's eyes grew frosty. "It might seem dumb to you, but that house was the place I had planned to make my forever home."

Roman's pulse thumped as Drake's confession rang in his ears. He couldn't believe Drake had refused the renovation project for such an inane reason. He chewed his lip.

Well, it's not that inane. I can see why he's upset. But

still, it's not like I bought the place to deliberately piss him off!

"I'm sorry," Roman said stiffly. "The realtor never said someone was interested in the mansion when I put in an offer."

"Would you have backed out if you'd known?" Drake said gruffly.

"No."

Drake scowled at Roman's blunt reply.

Roman hesitated. "I wanted that place as my forever home the moment I saw it too."

Drake's pupils flared. "You did?"

"Yeah." Roman raked his hair with a hand. "It's beautiful."

"It is that," Drake murmured.

A different kind of tension thickened the air between them as they gazed at one another.

"You said yes and no."

Drake blinked. "What?"

"Before. You said yes and no when I asked you if I was the reason you'd refused the contract."

Drake made a face. "Well, I can't say I was pleased to find out the person who'd bought the place was you."

Something sharp twisted inside Roman's chest. He swallowed.

"Is it because of what happened between us that one time?"

Drake sighed. "That. And the fact you're Roman Campbell."

"What does that mean?" Roman dug his nails into

his palms. "Are you saying you wouldn't have fucked me that night if you'd known who I was?"

"We didn't exactly fuck," Drake drawled. "And no. I would still have touched you."

Roman's pulse jumped at that. "So what, then?"

"I thought I would never see you again. And when I found out who you were, I was even more adamant that our paths never cross."

Confusion brought a frown to Roman's face. "I don't understand."

"You're trouble, Roman. With a capital T. It will be a conflict of interest if I were to work for you."

A buzzing noise filled Roman's ears. He barely registered Drake's last words, his whole being focused on the other man's first assertion.

That Roman was trouble.

A wave of pain and self-loathing choked Roman. Every mistake he'd made in the last thirteen years roared through his mind, starting with the one he would never forgive himself for. Roman clutched his chest, struggling to catch his breath under the deluge of memories threatening to drown him in despair.

He shuddered and focused on the exercises he'd learned in rehab to control the panic attack. Drake's voice reached him dimly through the ringing in his head. He froze when he felt Drake's hand on his arm.

"Don't," Roman mumbled. He blinked.

Drake's face finally came into focus.

"Are you okay?" The other man's eyes were dark with concern as he stared at Roman. "You've gone really pale."

"*Don't touch me!*" Roman yanked his arm from Drake's grip.

Drake recoiled as if he'd been slapped.

Roman's harsh pants echoed in the stillness as he finally managed to draw air inside his starving lungs.

"I'm sorry," Drake murmured. "I didn't mean to upset—"

"No," Roman spat out. "You've made your feelings perfectly clear. I won't bother you again." He twisted on his heels, stepped into the garden, and made for the gate at the back, angry at the way his body trembled.

CHAPTER EIGHT

SHIT.

Drake finished changing the oil in his Harley, rose to his feet, and cleaned his hands on a rag, a scowl dominating his face.

He couldn't stop thinking about what had happened last night.

The way Roman had reacted to his words had stunned him. He was aware the rockstar had gone through a rough time a few years back, when he'd had an epic melt down at an award ceremony in L.A. Drake had researched that incident at length that morning to find some clue as to why Roman had responded the way he had on that terrace.

After dozens of absurd and unproven speculations about the reasons behind Roman Campbell's longstanding addiction to drugs and alcohol and spectacular fall from grace, the entertainment world had finally decided he was simply a victim of his own success, like so many who were thrust into the limelight at a young age.

Except Drake didn't believe that. There was more to Roman than met the eye. Drake sensed a darkness deep inside the man that had evidently eaten at him one too many times in the past. A darkness Drake had glimpsed last night and that his callous words had unwittingly brought to the surface. Considering he had yet to fully conquer his own demons, this made Drake feel even more like a heartless bastard.

Yet, despite all his past mistakes, the world had welcomed Roman back with open arms when his band had made their comeback at the same event he'd trashed three years previously. Drake had watched a clip of their performance and couldn't help but smile at Roman's wry introduction when he'd taken to the stage. The crowd had roared with laughter when he'd mentioned his crass behavior the last time he'd been there and accepted his heartfelt apology with a round of applause.

But the confident man Drake had seen in that video and at Carter's wedding was not the person who'd faced Drake on that terrace last night. Instead, Roman had seemed like a wounded animal ready to snap at and bite anyone who approached him.

And I'm the one who made him that way.

Guilt twisted Drake's stomach all over again.

He hesitated before grabbing his keys and heading out.

Roman sipped his coffee morosely.

Forget about him. He obviously doesn't want to have anything to do with you.

Though he kept telling himself Drake was an asshole who didn't deserve his attention, Roman couldn't get the guy out of his mind. He sighed, pushed the memory of what happened yesterday firmly at the back of his mind, and squinted at the dazzling blue sky.

It was a beautiful Sunday afternoon. The sun warmed his face where he sat on the porch steps of his new home, the scent of wisteria lingering pleasantly in his nose, and the chatter of birds and the sounds of the forest filling his ears.

A faint smile curved Roman's lips despite his dark mood. He was more certain than ever now that buying this place had been the right thing to do. He had never felt so at peace with himself as he did right now.

The blissful silence was interrupted by the shrill ring of a cell. Roman took his phone out of his jeans and frowned at the caller ID.

"What do you want?"

"Is that any way to greet your lead guitarist?" Kurt Taylor drawled.

Roman pursed his lips. "I'm busy, Kurt. Get to the point."

"Ask him if he'd really staying in an RV!" someone shouted in the background.

Roman's frown deepened. "Is that Lewis?"

"Hugo and Robbie are here too," Kurt said. "James came over last night."

Roman swallowed a sigh. "Is he still harping on about me living in an RV for the next month?"

Kurt chuckled. "You know the guy. He's just worried about you."

"He told us we should take a break before we get back in the studio," Roman protested. "I'm just following his instructions."

"I don't think his instructions involved you buying a mansion in the middle of nowhere and renovating it."

Lewis Brandt, Crazyknot's drummer, came on the line. "You really staying in a motorhome right now, Romi?!"

Roman scowled at the diminutive.

"Why are you guys finding it so hard to believe that I'm renting an RV? None of us grew up in the lap of luxury. And FYI, this thing even has satellite TV."

"It's because you're Roman Campbell, dude." Lewis chuckled. "No one is gonna believe *the* Roman Campbell is camped out on the driveway of his new place living like a savage."

"I have a generator and running water, so it's not exactly the jungle out here," Roman snapped. "And maybe I should change my name. I'm getting sick and tired of people saying it like I'm some kind of freaking God!"

"But you are a god. You're the god of rock 'n' roll, dude."

Roman rolled his eyes hard.

Kurt took the phone off Lewis. "Sorry about that. Are you really okay?"

Roman bit back a sharp retort. He knew his friends

were only looking out for him. "Yeah, I am. I'll be back in a month."

"You're really not coming to L.A. for that whole time?" Kurt said, surprised. "Maybe we should head over one weekend—"

"Don't," Roman blurted. "The last thing this town needs is you guys barging into the place like you own it." The sound of an engine shattered the quiet around him. "I gotta go. Someone's coming."

Roman ignored Kurt's protest, ended the call, and climbed to his feet.

A black Harley came up the driveway and pulled to a stop next to his Ducati. Roman admired the sleek lines of the classic motorcycle for a moment before focusing on the driver. The man removed his helmet and ran a hand through his hair, tousling it farther.

Roman's heart thumped.

"Hi." Drake looked from the cup in Roman's hand to the shiny motorhome parked a short distance from the Ducati. "So, you're really staying on site?"

Roman ignored his racing pulse, pasted a cold expression on his face, and headed down the steps to the drive.

"What are you doing here?"

CHAPTER NINE

Drake masked a wince at Roman's icy tone.

I deserve that.

"I called Lara. She said you were planning to live here while the renovations got under way."

"That still doesn't answer my question," Roman said stiffly.

Drake sighed. "I'm sorry."

Roman blinked, surprise dawning on his face.

"I obviously upset you last night," Drake said quietly. "I was angry and I lashed out at you."

Roman clenched his hands, as if unsure how to respond.

"How about you show me around over a coffee?" Drake indicated the motorhome.

Roman chewed his lip.

Drake fought the impulse to walk over and tug the plump flesh free from the pretty, white teeth worrying it. Somehow, he wasn't surprised at the attraction he still felt for the rockstar.

Whatever this thing was between him and Roman, it wasn't going away anytime soon.

Roman finally reached a decision. "How do you take your coffee?"

Drake smiled at the reluctant white flag. "Black, one sugar." He hooked his helmet on the handlebar of his motorcycle and followed the rockstar into the RV.

The motorhome was bigger than it appeared from the outside and equipped with the latest high-tech gadgets, including a kitchenette that would put most homes in Twilight Falls to shame.

Drake explored the place curiously while Roman worked the coffee machine. A smile tugged at his lips when he saw the bedroom at the back.

I was right about those satin sheets.

"This is nice." He returned to the kitchen and took a seat at a black, granite table.

Roman shrugged and came over with Drake's drink and a fresh cup of coffee for himself. "It does the job." His knees brushed against Drake's when he sat opposite him.

"Still, I'd be careful about that generator," Drake said. "The squirrels might get to it."

Roman stared. A snort left him in the next instant. "Squirrels?!"

"You think I'm joking, but I've seen it happen many a times before," Drake said lightly.

"Yeah, well, we'll see about that," Roman chuckled.

His laughter made something warm bloom inside Drake's chest. This Roman was someone he hadn't seen before and he liked it. A lot.

Roman's expression slowly sobered, his irises darkening to a rich caramel at the sexual tension building between them.

Drake broke their locked stares and took a gulp of his coffee.

Damn. This guy is dangerous.

Roman cleared his throat. "So, what *are* you doing here?"

"I'm reconsidering your job offer."

Roman's pupils flared with surprise.

Drake gripped his cup tightly. The words had come out unbidden, surprising even him. He hadn't realized he'd been subconsciously thinking about taking on the contract until he'd just said so. Although common sense dictated he keep the hell away from this project and Roman, Drake couldn't stop himself from caring.

About the property he'd coveted for so long. And about the man who'd practically stolen it from him.

"Why?" Roman blurted. "I thought you said it was a bad idea."

"What I said was that it would lead to a conflict of interest."

Roman frowned. "How so?"

"Because I'm interested in you," Drake admitted steadily.

Roman inhaled sharply. Color stained his cheekbones.

Drake resisted the urge to lean over and touch his face to see if it felt as hot as it looked.

Really, really dangerous.

"What if I said I didn't mind?"

Roman's words hung between them, a question and a challenge.

For some reason he couldn't fathom, Drake felt a sharp pinch of disappointment.

"Are you saying you want to be sex friends?"

This time, the blush extended all the way to Roman's ears. "Maybe." He pursed his lips. "I'm not looking for anything serious, if that's what you're worried about."

"Neither am I." Drake wondered why the arrangement Roman was proposing irked him. After all, it was the way he liked his affairs. Short, hot, and with no strings attached.

"So, is that a yes?" Roman hazarded. "To the job, I mean," he added hastily.

Drake drank the rest of his coffee and took his time answering.

"I want to make something clear. *If* we hook up, it must not affect our working relationship."

"Alright." Roman hesitated and pursed his lips. "So, the sex friend thing is not a guarantee?"

Lust thickened Drake's cock at the chagrin in Roman's voice. "Should we test it out?"

Roman straightened in his chair. "Test what out?"

Drake rose, took their empty cups to the sink, and pulled Roman to his feet. "Consider this a trial run."

Roman sucked in air when Drake took hold of his waist and lifted him onto the edge of the table. Drake parted Roman's knees and stepped into the cradle of his thighs. The mocha eyes opposite him clouded over with desire.

"Drake," Roman breathed.

Roman's trembling voice shot straight to Drake's groin. He lifted gentle hands to Roman's face, angled his head, and took his mouth with his own.

CHAPTER TEN

Roman shuddered and clung to Drake's shoulders, body straining closer to the other man. This kiss was different from the ones they'd shared that first night.

It was soft and slow and sweet and it was going to drive Roman out of his mind.

Drake brushed his lips carefully across Roman's over and over again, as if committing their shape to memory. It wasn't until Roman made a demanding noise at the back of throat that Drake finally gave him what he wanted and swept his tongue inside his mouth.

Roman's dick hardened as Drake frenched him with masterful skill. The world faded around him, his entire being focusing on the man holding him with aching tenderness and kissing him like he was the most precious thing in the world.

Drake's fingers and tongue grew more urgent as he surrendered to the passion burning between them. Roman moaned, pleasure surging through him with every suck and nip of Drake's clever tongue and teeth.

Drake broke their kiss and skimmed his hands playfully down Roman's neck. He paused on the pulse beating furiously at the base of Roman's throat and caressed it for tantalizing seconds before nudging Roman's chin up and brushing his lips over Roman's tattoo, his tongue darting out to lick and taste Roman's skin as he explored the dark swirls.

Roman groaned, blood thundering in his ears and his cock growing damp with precum. He couldn't believe he was so close to exploding with just a kiss.

Drake's fingers found Roman's nipple ring and gave it a playful twist.

"*Ah!*" Roman hissed and arched his back at the pleasure-pain.

Drake pulled away slightly, eyes blazing with lust. He yanked Roman's T-shirt out of his jeans, tugged it over his head, and cast it on the bench next to the table. He stilled when he saw Roman's naked chest.

"Beautiful." Drake trailed callused fingers reverently down Roman's torso and back up again, his rough touch igniting sparks on Roman's skin. "You're so fucking beautiful."

Roman shuddered when Drake leaned down and took his left nipple into his mouth, his tongue and teeth playing and tugging on the metal ring while his stubble grazed Roman's sensitive skin. He pressed one hand against the table behind him and grabbed Drake's head with the other as Drake lavished his flesh with torrid kisses and explored his body with his hands and mouth.

Roman's belly clenched when Drake turned his

attention to his abs. Drake lowered himself onto his knees and kissed the strip of downy hair arrowing down from Roman's belly button, his fingers making Roman's muscles quiver in anticipation as he traced the deep V leading to Roman's groin over and over again.

Roman's pants grew loud and harsh when Drake unbuckled his belt and snapped open the top button of his jeans, their heated gazes locked. The sound of Drake pulling down the zipper made Roman bite down on his lip. He watched breathlessly as Drake worked his erection free from his boxer shorts.

"This part of you is pretty too." Drake caressed the rosy, glistening head of Roman's cock with a thumb. "I'm glad I'm getting to see it in the daylight." He leaned down and circled his tongue lazily across Roman's over sensitive skin.

"Fuck!" Roman bucked his hips.

"Is that what you want, Roman?" Drake spread Roman's thighs wide and danced his mouth up and down Roman's trembling shaft, his lips skimming Roman's cock teasingly. "You want me to fuck you with my mouth?"

"Yes!" Roman begged, unheeding of how desperate he sounded. He rolled his cock against Drake's mouth. "Please! I need you to—*Oh, Jesus fuck!*"

ROMAN'S CRY ECHOED AGAINST THE CONFINES OF THE RV as Drake finally gave him what he wanted and took him inside his mouth.

Drake's pulse thrummed when he tasted Roman's salty skin and precum. Roman's musky scent and trimmed pubes teased his nose and made his own erection twitch painfully as he carefully swallowed Roman's rock-hard shaft to the back of his throat.

Drake hastily freed his own dick and gave it a brisk rub as he started blowing Roman the way he liked it. Roman fisted a hand in Drake's hair and thrust his hips, his own mouth open on low, sensual moans as he matched Drake's motions.

"So good!" Roman gasped, his movements growing increasingly frantic as he neared his climax. "Drake! I'm gonna—*I'm gonna come!*"

Roman went rigid above Drake, his breath hitching. He exploded on a loud curse, his cock throbbing and filling Drake's hungry mouth with hot cum. Drake pressed the heel of his palm against Roman's lower belly as he convulsed deliciously above him.

Roman grunted and groaned, balls spasming and cock jerking as the motion intensified and drew out his pleasure. By the time Drake pulled off Roman's dick, he was a hot, whimpering mess.

"Salty *and* sweet," Drake teased, flicking the head of Roman's trembling cock with his tongue as he let go of the pleasantly spent organ.

Roman shivered and moaned, body limp where he'd propped himself on his elbows. Drake rose and reached for the bottle of olive oil on the kitchen counter.

Roman's eyes widened when he saw Drake's raging erection.

He swallowed. "You're big."

Drake chuckled, the action making his swollen cock ache. "I'm gonna choose to take that as a compliment. Now, come here." He tugged Roman to his feet, stripped him of his jeans and shoes, and turned him so he faced the other way. "Put your hands on the table."

Roman shuddered and did as he was told. He looked over his shoulder and worried his lip with his teeth when Drake went down on his knees behind him. Drake palmed Roman's ass, massaged the taut muscles, and kissed and nipped at Roman's hot, quivering skin, readying him for what he intended to do.

Roman hummed and arched his back when Drake finally parted his cleft and exposed his hole, his dick hard again.

"Fuck." Drake's erection throbbed hungrily when he saw Roman's pink pucker. "Every inch of you is goddamn beautiful."

Roman cried out when Drake flicked his hole with his tongue. He jerked and writhed as Drake teased and circled the twitching folds, Drake's hands holding him firmly in place. Drake spent time softening Roman's entrance before stretching him open and working his furrowed tongue inside Roman's body.

"Aaaah!"

The way Roman shouted and the precum dripping from his stiff cock told Drake he was close to another orgasm. Drake's belly tightened as he fought back his own climax, eager to enjoy Roman's sinful taste for as long as he could.

"More," Roman moaned. "I want more!"

Drake cursed and grabbed the olive oil. He coated

two fingers liberally, parted Roman's hole, and pushed inside. Roman groaned and curled his toes, pleasure stiffening his body.

Drake climbed to his feet as he plundered Roman's passage with deep, steady thrusts, his fingertips finding and probing the soft bump of Roman's prostate. Roman went wild, hoarse cries ripping from his throat as he danced back on Drake's hand, chasing his pleasure.

Drake pushed his turgid cock under Roman's balls and punched his shaft repeatedly between Roman's hot thighs, mimicking what he was dying to do to him.

Roman grabbed his cock and started rubbing himself.

Drake made a savage noise, curled a hand around Roman's throat, and pulled him up until Roman's back practically kissed his chest. Roman moaned when the new angle brought Drake's erection flush against his dripping dick. He twisted his head and frantically sought Drake's mouth while Drake continued finger fucking his twitching hole and driving his erection between his thighs.

Drake's orgasm tightened his belly and danced down his spine as he kissed Roman, swallowing the other man's moans and gasps. Roman reached down and closed a hand on Drake's erection. He stared into Drake's eyes and rubbed Drake's aching flesh, pupils dilated with passion and face flushed with pleasure.

An animal groan left Drake when he finally came, his climax sending blood roaring in his skull while he filled Roman's eager hand with his cum, his hips lifting

Roman's body as he thrust powerfully. Roman shivered and jerked when his orgasm finally claimed him, his groans and whimpers echoing sweetly in Drake's ears.

They collapsed on the table a moment later, their pants loud and their hearts thundering against one another where their bodies touched.

"I think we can safely say the trial run was a success," Roman mumbled.

Drake chuckled and kissed Roman's damp nape.

CHAPTER ELEVEN

Lara stared as Drake and his men pulled up the private driveway in a line of trucks and vans.

"What the hell did you do to convince him to accept the contract?"

Roman scratched his cheek awkwardly where he stood beside her. He couldn't exactly say he and Drake were intending to trade sexual favors for the duration of this project. He suppressed the torrid images from his and Drake's intimate encounter in the RV over the weekend and pasted a vague expression on his face.

"I can be quite persuasive when I try."

Lara glanced at him skeptically before strolling down to meet the men.

It had taken Drake two days to assemble the crew he needed to start work on the mansion. Considering the brief notice and Drake's ongoing commitments to his other clients, Roman considered this a miracle.

Some of the guys with Drake stared at Roman with tongue-tied awe as their boss made introductions in a proficient, business-like voice Roman shouldn't have found attractive but did.

And why the hell does he look so hot in cargo pants and a plaid shirt?!

Drake's pewter-colored trousers and checkered white and blue flannel shirt accentuated his tall frame and powerful build, reminding Roman of the wickedly sensual acts they had engaged in recently. Roman chastised himself for the filthy direction his thoughts had taken and eyed the last man Drake introduced.

Gary Bartlett, Drake's foreman, seemed unaffected by Roman's fame and met his gaze squarely.

"Gary will be in charge of the construction site on the days I'm not able to be here," Drake explained as they headed up the steps to the mansion's porch, oblivious to Roman discreetly ogling the way his ass filled his work pants. "Now, how about we take an official tour of the place and you two tell us what you have in mind?"

To Roman's surprise, Drake included his entire team as they walked around the property and its outbuildings, Lara apprising them of the plans she and Roman had put together. The architect seemed used to Drake's way of working and used her tablet to show them visual projections of every room.

Drake and Gary asked questions and made several suggestions as they progressed through the detailed inspection, the foreman and his two assistants taking notes on their own tablets.

By the time they returned to the porch, Roman's mind was reeling. He'd known renovating the mansion would be a complex undertaking. The sheer volume of details Lara and Drake had just discussed made him realize just how complicated and time consuming bringing the place to its former glory was going to be.

Lara smiled faintly when she clocked his anxious expression. "If it's any consolation, most clients feel the way you're feeling right now before the start of a project."

"Really?" Roman murmured. "'Cause I get the impression we're about to build a rocket, not renovate a mansion."

Several of the men laughed at that, their faces more relaxed than they had been at the start of the tour now that they'd realized Roman was a mere mortal.

Lara glanced at Drake.

"Well, you're in safe hands, so try not to worry too much," she told Roman kindly.

Drake hung back while the architect and his team headed down the steps. "Can we talk inside for a minute?" He indicated the main entrance and the hallway beyond.

"Sure," Roman murmured, curious. They headed inside the mansion. "What did you want to talk—"

ROMAN'S QUESTION ENDED ON A GASP WHEN DRAKE yanked him close and pushed him against the wall next to the sidelight. The rockstar barely had time to draw breath before Drake took his mouth in a demanding kiss.

Roman stiffened before melting against Drake, his arms rising to loop possessively around Drake's neck and pull him closer. A shudder ran through Drake as he reveled in Roman's intoxicating taste. He couldn't believe it had only been two days since he'd last kissed him.

Lust burned brightly through Drake's veins by the time he reluctantly let go of Roman's lips, Roman's glazed expression going some way toward satisfying the hunger twisting Drake's belly.

"I could have sworn you said something about keeping things professional when you were on site," Roman mumbled, the tips of his ears flushed a pretty pink.

Drake swallowed a groan.

Shit. I wonder if his dick has gone the same shade.

He pushed that alluring thought firmly to the back of his mind and frowned at Roman.

"Did you know your piercing is visible through that T-shirt?"

Roman blinked before glancing at his chest. The way he fingered his nipple ring made Drake want to yank his shirt up and go to town on the hard nub.

This guy is gonna make me lose my fucking mind!

"Does it bother you?" Roman's lips quirked in a playful smile, his teasing expression telling Drake he knew exactly what Drake was thinking right now.

"Yes," Drake groaned. "I don't want other guys looking at your body."

Roman's mouth fell open. He burst out laughing.

"I can't believe you just said that!"

Drake palmed Roman's ass and tugged him so that their groins kissed. Roman bit his lip when he registered the fullness of Drake's cock, the laughter fading from his face, only to be replaced by desire.

"Let me make something clear. I don't like sharing." Drake leaned down and nipped Roman's left earlobe with his teeth. "You're mine while we're in this relationship."

Roman shivered and twisted his neck, exposing his skin farther. "I am?"

"Yup." Drake nuzzled the whirls of Roman's ear and teased them with his tongue. "Also, you seem to have forgotten something. I love this mansion, so I'm going to do everything I can to make sure I deliver on this project, so relax." He pulled back, his expression turning serious. "I've got you."

Roman's pupils flared slightly at Drake's words. He hesitated.

"Did you like the plans Lara and I drew up?"

Drake smiled. "Yes. They are pretty much what I would have chosen to do to the place."

Roman flushed, looking pleased. "They are?"

"Yeah." Drake arched an eyebrow. "I was pretty shocked. I wouldn't have put you down for being so traditional in your tastes."

Roman pursed his lips. "Wait. So, you're saying you thought I was some kind of ultra-fashionable city hick with no appreciation for the finer things in life?"

Drake resisted the urge to kiss the pouty mouth so close to his own. "Something like that."

Roman narrowed his eyes. "You know, I might not

put out the next time you want to get down and dirty." He stared when Drake laughed out loud.

"Sorry." Drake chuckled and pressed a light kiss to Roman's forehead. "You just reminded me of something a friend said. By the way, they're predicting heavy rain tonight, so mind that generator. I'll have my electrician hook up an outlet socket for your RV tomorrow, when we start working on site."

"I'm sure it'll be fine," Roman murmured dismissively.

CHAPTER TWELVE

THIS IS **SO** *NOT FINE.*

Roman cursed his own foolishness as he fumbled around in the dark. He'd come into the bedroom to grab the charging cable for his phone when the lights had gone out.

It took a moment for him to realize he couldn't hear the hum of the portable generator above the sound of the rain pounding the RV. He made his way to the window, swore when he knocked his shin against something sharp, and parted the blinds.

Spray from the heavy downpour misted the air, reducing visibility farther. He squinted and made out the shadowy shape of the engine where it sat on the drive.

The main indicator light was off.

Shit!

The first ripple of a panic attack twisted Roman's gut. He took a shallow breath and forced his quickening heart to slow down as he made his way to the main living area.

He hated the dark.

Roman's heart sank when he grabbed his phone from the couch. Though he had signal, the battery was dangerously low. He'd put off charging it the whole day, too absorbed in writing the new song he'd come up with that afternoon.

He pocketed his cell, shrugged into a hooded jacket, and took a flashlight from the emergency kit in one of the kitchen cupboards.

Thank God James made sure the RV was kitted out with one before he left.

He stepped out of the RV and made his way to the generator. The cause of the power failure became all too clear when he shone the flashlight over it.

Something had frayed the cable connecting it to the RV.

You gotta be shitting me!

Roman recalled Drake's warning about squirrels and scowled at the nearby trees. He stood frozen for an indecisive moment, rain pummeling him and soaking his jeans and shoes.

Staying inside the vehicle in the dark would only make him more claustrophobic. His only options were to check into a hotel in town, or ask Lara or Drake for help. He ruled out the hotel straightaway.

He didn't want the whole of Twilight Falls knowing about the incident.

Besides, knowing my luck, the paparazzi will be camped outside the place by the morning.

Roman swallowed a sigh. Lara was struggling with a teething toddler at and not getting much sleep lately. Which left Drake.

Roman frowned and trudged back to the RV.

He couldn't call Drake. Not only would the builder tell him "I told you so," it would feel awkward to step in Drake's territory uninvited.

Roman grabbed a pillow, blankets, a couple of towels, and some dry clothes before stuffing them all inside a clean trash bag. He found his phone charger, tucked it inside his jacket, and raced up the shallow stairs to the mansion, the flashlight bobbing wildly in his hand.

A curse left him when he tripped on the last step. The flashlight flew out of his hand and smashed against the wall as he went down. Pain burned his left palm and knee. Roman stayed still for a stunned moment before climbing shakily to his feet.

Blood oozed out from the fresh graze on his hand. He could feel the sting of a wound on his leg.

Great. Just great.

Roman scowled when he lifted the flashlight. It was broken.

Shadows greeted him when he entered the house. He switched on the naked bulb James had put up in the hallway and breathed a sigh of relief as the gloom abated.

Roman headed into what had once been the impeccable main drawing room of the mansion, made himself a bed on the only couch in the place, and plugged his phone in a nearby power outlet. By the time he'd changed out of his wet clothes, he was shivering.

The temperature had plummeted with the rain storm.

Roman slipped under the covers of his makeshift bed and curled into a ball. He gripped his cell phone like a life line, the glow from the screen a reassuring presence in the twilight bathing the room.

It's only for one night. Besides, I've survived worse than this.

Lightning flashed outside. Thunder boomed an instant later, the sound so loud it rattled the windows and made Roman jump.

The light flickered and went out in the hallway. Roman's cell phone died.

Darkness swallowed him, bringing with it an all too familiar terror.

WATER SWISHED HEAVILY UNDER THE WHEELS OF DRAKE'S Jeep as he rode up the mountain. The private access road leading to the Strickland Estate appeared in the headlights a short while later. He turned into it and soon reached the new security gate guarding the driveway.

Dread knotted Drake's stomach as he wound the window down and punched in the code.

He hadn't been able to stop thinking about Roman

since the storm erupted over the valley an hour ago. He'd told himself he was being a fool a dozen times over before he finally decided to put his mind at rest and call Roman.

A dark foreboding had gripped him when he hadn't been able to get through to Roman's cell phone. He was out of his house and headed over to Roman's before he knew it, his heart pounding with an unnamed fear.

Drake clenched his teeth when he rounded the bend in the drive and saw the dark RV. He parked next to Roman's Ducati, stepped out into the rain, and ran over to the motorhome.

"Roman! Are you in there?!" he shouted, pounding the door.

There was no reply.

Drake cursed and tried the door handle. His pulse stuttered when it opened. Silence and shadows greeted him as he climbed the steps, his heart in his throat.

"Roman?"

Drake's voice echoed around the empty motorhome. He tried the light switch unsuccessfully.

Generator must have died!

Drake exited the RV and grabbed his flashlight from the Jeep. A quick inspection of the generator confirmed his suspicions. He rose from his haunches and stared around the dark estate.

Where the hell is he?

Drake's gaze found the hulking shape of the mansion on the hill. He headed rapidly up the steps and stormed inside the gloom-filled hallway.

"Roman? Are you in here?"

A faint sound reached him from farther down the hall. Drake followed it to the main drawing room.

Someone was on the corner of the old, stained couch. Drake stiffened when his flashlight washed over the figure sitting with his knees hugged to his chest and his body curled into a tight ball.

Roman rocked slightly to and fro, his eyes closed and his face ashen. He was gripping his cell phone so tightly his knuckles blanched. A low mumble fell from his lips like a prayer.

"It's okay! It's gonna be okay, Ash!" Roman repeated over and over again, his breathing fast and shallow.

Drake wondered at the name as he made his way carefully to the couch.

He knew a panic attack when he saw one.

He knelt in front of Roman and gently touched his hand.

Damn. He's ice cold.

"Roman?"

It was almost a minute before Roman registered Drake's presence. He blinked his eyes open and stared at Drake, his gaze gradually growing focused.

"Drake?" he mumbled tremulously. "Is that—" he paused and swallowed, "—is that really you?!"

"Yes." Drake grazed Roman's cheek with his knuckles. "I'm not going anywhere."

Roman's breath hitched. He launched himself at Drake, almost knocking him to the floor. Drake's heart twisted as Roman wrapped his arms tightly around him.

He could feel the shudders racking Roman's body

and the hot wetness of Roman's tears soaking into his neck.

Drake hugged Roman to his chest, his mind full of questions.

What the hell is going on?!

CHAPTER THIRTEEN

Roman stared blindly at the wall of Drake's bathroom, hot steam curling around him. Memories stained in blood faded from his mind as his body slowly warmed up.

The bath was going some way toward taking away the bitter cold chilling his bones. He didn't think there would be as easy a cure for the numbness gripping his heart in its icy clutches.

Only two things could alleviate that pain.

Unfortunately, he'd sworn off both eighteen months ago.

Roman sighed, rubbed his hand down his face, and winced when he inadvertently rubbed his wound.

Drake walked into the bathroom with a pile of clothes and a towel.

"How are you feeling?"

Roman gave him a laconic smile. "Like a fool."

Drake put the clothes on the counter. "You have

nothing to feel foolish about. You can't exactly control a panic attack."

Roman swallowed when Drake knelt by the clawfoot bathtub and carefully took his hand. "I meant that more about the squirrels and the generator."

A faint smile curved Drake's lips as he examined the grazes on Roman's hand and knee. "Well, you're not wrong there."

A shiver danced down Roman's spine at Drake's gentle touch.

Drake met his gaze. "Cold?"

Roman bit his lip and shook his head.

Drake looked down and clocked Roman's stirring erection through the water. "Let me make one thing clear. Nothing is gonna happen between us tonight."

Disappointment shot through Roman at Drake's firm tone.

"Why not?" he retorted, not caring that he sounded like a petulant kid.

Drake frowned. "Because you've just suffered some kind of trauma. I'm not going to take advantage of you when you're not thinking clearly."

"My dick is thinking clearly," Roman muttered. "And you won't be taking advantage of me."

"Yeah, well, your dick has a life of its own. Now, up you come."

Roman spluttered when Drake pulled him to his feet and folded the large bath towel around him. "I can dry myself!"

Drake arched an eyebrow. "Can I watch?"

Roman frowned. "Blow me, Jackson."

"I believe I've done that a couple of times already," Drake teased.

Roman's frown turned into a full-blown scowl.

Drake laughed. "Alright, alright." He backed away with his hands raised. "Come join me in the lounge when you're done. I need to take care of your wounds."

A fuzzy feeling warmed Roman's chest as he dried himself and put on the sweatpants and T-shirt Drake had brought him. They were one size too big and hung off his body. Roman rolled up the hems of the soft sweats and hesitated before sniffing the T-shirt, wondering if it still smelled like Drake.

He flushed when he realized what he was doing. He hastily balled his clothes and dropped them in the laundry basket.

Shit. I'm acting like some kind of stalker.

Drake was standing in front of the fireplace dominating the sunken floor when Roman came out into the living room. Flames crackled in the open hearth, the fire casting flickering, orange light across Drake's pensive face as he drank from a cup.

"Your house is something else."

Drake looked over his shoulder and watched Roman come down the steps. "Thanks."

"How long have you had this place?"

Roman looked around curiously as he padded barefoot across the floor. Considering Drake's interest in the Strickland Estate, his home wasn't at all what Roman had imagined it to be.

The modern, single story, flat-roof building was made entirely of wood and glass, with clean, crisp lines

Roman couldn't help but admire. The interior was even more fascinating, with an eclectic collection of furniture and expensive art pieces providing splashes of color against the dark, masculine decor. The open plan living-slash-dining area and kitchen taking up most of the rear of the house boasted a floor to ceiling glass wall overlooking a graveled backyard and a dark forest.

Drake handed Roman the steaming cup sitting on the mantelpiece. "Five years."

"You built it yourself?"

"Uh-huh."

Roman sipped the drink and paused. "Is this hot cocoa?"

"I thought you could do with warming up." Drake smiled faintly and headed over to one of the black leather couches dominating the space.

Roman joined him. "Yeah, well, I know something else that would warm me up even better, but someone's not willing to cooperate."

Drake chuckled as he opened the first aid kit on the coffee table. "I'm not a villain."

Roman eyed him sideways as he applied antiseptic to the graze on Roman's palm with a wad of clean gauze. He bit his lip at the mild sting.

"I know. If you were a villain, I'd be flat on my back, getting fucked right now."

Drake snorted. He taped a breathable dressing on Roman's palm and pulled up the leg of Roman's sweatpants so he could take care of Roman's knee.

Roman did his best to ignore Drake's electric touch

and the alluring way the firelight softened his face and highlighted his mouth. A series of torrid images suddenly flashed before his eyes. Of Drake's lips on his body. Of Drake sucking his cock and hungrily swallowing his cum. Of Drake's wicked tongue teasing his hole.

Roman pushed the filthy visions firmly to the back of his head.

Jesus, I'm acting like a horny teenager!

"Do you always say the first thing that comes to your mind?" Drake glanced up at Roman from beneath his lashes as he cleaned the graze.

"It's a bad habit James is trying to rid me of. I can literally see his blood pressure rise when I do a live interview."

Drake smiled and finished dressing Roman's knee. "He really looks after you, huh?"

Roman leaned his head back on the couch. "Yeah. They all do."

"They?"

"The rest of my band." Roman made a face. "I'm like the unofficial baby of the group. They're always mothering me."

"Does it frustrate you?"

Roman blinked at Drake's question. "No. And I didn't mean to sound ungrateful," he added hastily. "It…it makes me happy that they care so much. And I feel truly…cherished." Heat flooded his cheeks at the confession. He avoided Drake's gaze and took a sip of his cocoa. "I'm curious about something."

"What?"

"If I'm not wrong, I've only met six of the Terrible Seven. Who's the seventh guy?"

Drake raised an eyebrow. "Carter never told you about Miles?"

Roman shook his head, puzzled. "No."

"I guess he wouldn't really have had a reason to tell you what happened back then," Drake muttered.

Roman's curiosity deepened.

Drake hesitated. "Miles is still around. It's just—he never woke up after the accident." He sighed at Roman's mystified expression. "Miles Martinez is the seventh member of the Terrible Seven. A drunk driver crashed into Alex's mom's truck on the fourth of July, when we'd gone up the mountains to go watch the fireworks. We were eighteen at the time." Drake fisted his hands, a frown marring his brow. "The six of us got out of the wreck pretty much unscathed. Miles suffered a head injury. He was in a coma for a while. And he just—" he paused and swallowed, "—he never opened his eyes again."

Roman put his cup down and closed a hand over Drake's knuckles. "I'm sorry."

Drake nodded wordlessly. It was a moment before he spoke.

"Can I ask you something?"

"Sure," Roman murmured.

"Who's Ash?" Drake said quietly.

CHAPTER FOURTEEN

DRAKE SILENTLY CURSED HIMSELF WHEN THE COLOR drained from Roman's face.

"How do you—how do you know that name?!" Roman's expression had turned haunted once more.

Drake wondered if he shouldn't have asked the question. He steeled himself in the next instant. He wasn't going to be of any help to Roman if he stayed quiet.

And he wanted to help him. He wanted to take away the pain and heartache that had dulled Roman's eyes and turned his body to ice when he'd come upon him in the mansion tonight.

"You were mumbling it when I found you."

Roman's eyes widened. "I—I was?"

Drake dipped his chin. "Yeah. You kept saying, 'It's okay. It's gonna be okay, Ash.'"

Air left Roman in a soft whoosh. He stared blindly at the floor, his face stunned. "I hadn't realized."

"You wouldn't have. You were in the middle of a full-blown panic attack."

Roman winced at that.

It was Drake's turn to hold Roman's hands. "All I'm saying is I'm here if you want to talk about it. You might feel better if you do."

For a moment, Drake thought Roman would refuse his offer.

"There's something you should know before I tell you more." Roman worriedly his lip with his teeth as he stared at Drake, his expression troubled.

"I'm listening."

"What I'm about to reveal has been banned from disclosure to the public by the courts."

Surprise jolted Drake. He hadn't been expecting that. "What?"

"What happened to me falls under a domestic violence protection order," Roman continued in a stilted voice. "The only ones who know the truth are James, my lawyers, and the other members of Crazyknot."

Drake's pulse quickened. "Don't you need your lawyers' permission before you—"

"No." Roman shook his head. "Now that I'm no longer a juvenile, I can disclose this information to whomever I choose, at my own discretion."

The fact that Roman was choosing to trust him with sensitive legal information about his past made Drake's chest tighten with a nameless emotion.

Roman inhaled shakily. "It was the dark." His

fingers trembled where Drake held them. "That's why I panicked tonight."

Drake resisted the instinct to take Roman in his arms and waited patiently.

"We hated the dark," Roman murmured, staring blindly into space. "Ashley more than me."

Drake frowned. He hadn't come across that name when he'd read up on Roman a few days back.

"Ashley?"

Roman hesitated before nodding shakily. "Yeah. Ashley was my sister." He swallowed convulsively. "My twin."

Drake drew a sharp breath at the despair darkening Roman's eyes. He gave in to the voice telling him to hold Roman and folded him gently into his arms. "Was? She's dead?"

Roman nodded wordlessly. He clutched at Drake's shoulders and buried his face in Drake's chest, seeking his heat. Drake clenched his jaw, his touch gentle as he stroked Roman's back with soothing motions. The feel of Roman's thundering heart and quivering body made him want to punch whoever had hurt him so badly.

In that moment, Drake realized he didn't want to let Roman go right now. That he wanted to protect him from a past that still haunted him to this day.

"How did she die?"

"She killed herself. We'd just turned fifteen at the time."

Drake froze.

Roman's voice had gone lifeless.

"Our dad was a drunk and a gambler. And he used

his fists more than his mouth when he was in a foul mood, which was pretty much every day."

Drake's pulse quickened, his own demons stirring as Roman's words came pouring out of the dark place inside him.

"Our mom left a few days before our birthday. She upped and disappeared one night, without saying a word to either of us." Bitterness colored Roman's words. "Our dad's drinking got worse after that. He was clever. He never hit us where it showed, even when we were kids. His favorite thing back then was to lock us up in a closet in the backroom. We were five when he first did it. I remember Ashley screaming so loudly her voice stayed hoarse for an entire week. The only reason I managed to endure it was because she was with me. Still, the two of us had always hated the dark since that time."

Anger rushed through Drake. He tightened his arms reflexively around Roman. Roman squeezed back, his hot breath warming Drake's skin through his shirt. He shuddered in Drake's arms.

"She just woke up one day and had enough. I was at school when it happened. She said she had a headache and wanted to stay home. Our dad had already left for work." A humorless chuckle fell from Roman's lips. "You know how people claim a twin can always sense what's happening to his other half? Well, that wasn't the case with me. She was stone cold when I walked into our house and found her. She'd cut her wrist with a kitchen knife."

"Did he—" Drake paused and swallowed, "—did

your father ever?" He stopped, too scared to voice the rest of his question.

"If you mean, did our dad abuse us sexually, then the answer is no." Roman pulled away slightly and met Drake's gaze. "He used to call me his little faggot and he told Ashley she was a whore. But he never looked at us that way."

Drake suppressed his fury and caressed Roman's cheek with his knuckles. "Where's your dad now?"

A mirthless half-smile tilted Roman's lips. "Rotting in jail. Remember how I said he was a gambler? Well, he embezzled a quarter of a million dollars from his company funds. The police arrested him a week after Ashley's funeral. Once they saw my bruises and had a psychologist interview me, they also charged him with child abuse. He took a plea deal so the case never went to trial."

"God." Drake took a deep breath and pressed a kiss to Roman's forehead, his mind a riot of emotions. "I'm so sorry, Roman."

"It's not your fault," Roman mumbled against Drake's throat.

Drake digested what Roman had told him in the soft silence that fell between them. He still couldn't believe Roman had put his faith so squarely in him.

"What happened to you afterward? Did you have relatives take you in?"

Roman shook his head. "We never had much to do with my mom or my dad's families. They were strangers to us. I ended up in a children's home."

Drake clenched his teeth. Even though his own

childhood had hardly been a bed of roses, at least he'd had a roof over his head and food on the table. He couldn't imagine how lost and abandoned Roman must have felt at such a crucial age.

"It was the best thing that happened to me. Because that's where I met them and my fortunes changed."

Drake stared, puzzled. "Them?"

"The guys who I would form Crazyknot with, and James. We were in the same children's home." Roman smiled genuinely this time. "We were like cats and dogs at first, and we got into more fist fights than I can count. One of our social workers got fed up with us, gave us some old musical instruments, and confined us to a garage for a day so we could bond. Turns out we were all naturals. Well, except for James." He grimaced. "That guy couldn't string a guitar or sing a tune if his life depended on it."

Drake chuckled.

Roman grinned. "But he was amazing at getting us gigs, so we made him our manager pretty much straight after we left the home. We haven't regretted it since." His smile faded. "It was James who advised me to change my name before we officially launched the band. He thought it would be a good way to turn my back on my past."

Drake hesitated. "The alcohol and the drugs? Was that all about Ashley?"

Roman stiffened slightly before relaxing in Drake's arms once more. "Yes. Most of it was. I was angry. Had been angry for such a long time I couldn't recall a day when I didn't wake up to the burning rage I'd lived with for so long. I was mad at my dad for ruining our lives. I hated my mom for abandoning us." A trace of bitterness underscored Roman's voice again. "And I resented Ash, for leaving me all alone. I wanted to forget it all, and the booze and drugs helped me do that."

Drake was quiet for a while. "Did you manage to work through those feelings when you were in rehab?" he finally said.

Roman drew back and frowned. "How do you know about that?"

Drake scratched his cheek, embarrassed. "I kinda looked you up before I came to your place last Sunday."

Roman arched an eyebrow. "Are you my stalker now?"

"A stalker wouldn't have refused to have sex with you," Drake replied sedately.

Roman pursed his lips. "You're right." He sighed and snuggled into Drake's arms, making Drake's belly tighten with more than just the need to comfort him. "And the answer to your question is yes. But I still suffer from the panic attacks. They don't happen nearly as often as they used to though."

The fire crackled loudly in the hush that followed.

"Thank you," Drake finally said. "For trusting me with all of that." He felt Roman smile against his chest.

"I couldn't exactly say no to my knight in shining armor. Or should I say my knight with the magic flashlight?"

Drake groaned. "That was a terrible joke."

Roman chuckled. "So terrible."

"The worst," Drake affirmed. "Come on, let me show you the guest bedroom. We both need to get some sleep."

Roman's face fell as Drake let go of him and collected their cold drinks. "We're really not doing it?"

It took all of Drake's willpower to resist the sweet temptation that was Roman in that moment. "If by 'it' you mean sex, then no."

"Alright," Roman grumbled as he rose and followed Drake into the kitchen. "But I draw the line at sleeping in the guest bedroom. I'm gonna sleep with you."

"I don't think that's a great idea," Drake said.

"Why not?" Roman challenged.

"Because, for all I know, you'll jump me in the middle of the night," Drake said, poker-faced.

Roman gasped. "Why you—!" He scowled. "You really think you're that hard to resist?!"

Drake laughed and kissed the tip of Roman's nose. "That's three times now that you've asked me to have sex with you."

"What do you mean, three times?!" Roman said, aghast.

Drake dried his hands and counted on his fingers. "There was that one time on Sunday, in the RV. Then tonight, in the bathroom. And just—"

"Alright, alright!" Roman snapped. "Sheesh!"

CHAPTER FIFTEEN

Roman woke up to a pair of hard arms wrapped around his waist and the feel of Drake's body pressed snugly against his own.

He stayed still for a moment as he stared at Drake, not daring to move.

His eyelashes are so long.

Drake's face was relaxed and youthful in his sleep, the crow's feet framing his eyes and the lines wrinkling his brow faint against his tanned skin. His wide chest rose and feel shallowly with his breaths and his long legs were intimately entangled with Roman's.

Roman pursed his lips as he scanned Drake's magnificent form.

Shame he's wearing pajamas.

He was wondering if he would get away with sneaking a peek inside Drake's pants when Drake stirred and opened his eyes.

Drake's irises darkened to a grey cobalt when he registered Roman's presence in his bed. "Good morning." He leaned down and nuzzled his nose against Roman's. "Did you sleep well?"

Roman swallowed a groan at Drake's sexy, husky voice.

Morning Drake was dangerous.

"I did, thank you."

Roman was surprised to find this wasn't a lie. Although he'd thought he wouldn't be able to sleep with Drake last night due to everything that had happened *and* the ever-present sexual tension between them, he'd passed out the moment his head had hit the pillow.

"Good." Drake smiled faintly. "Now, should we do something about *that*?"

Roman blinked. "Do something about what?"

"Hmm." Drake brushed his lips teasingly across Roman's mouth. "Correct me if I'm wrong, Mr. Campbell, but I do believe that's your very erect dick poking my thigh."

Roman shivered and pressed closer to Drake, seeking his lips. "What can I say? I'm just a healthy man with morning wood."

Drake drew back and arched an eyebrow. "So, you're saying you'd be like this with just about anyone in your bed?"

Roman grinned and moved up to tug on Drake's lower lip with his teeth. "Is that jealousy I hear in your voice?"

Drake groaned and pinned Roman under his body.

"You're such a tease," he mumbled against Roman's mouth, his eyes burning bright with desire.

Roman rolled his hips and chuckled when the sensual movement earned him another heartfelt groan. "I just know what I want."

Drake swallowed Roman's laughter with his mouth, his tongue parting Roman's lips to sweep possessively inside.

Roman moaned when Drake aligned their bodies and stroked his rock-hard cock against Roman's dick with delicious punches of his hips. The feeling of Drake's tongue lashing passionately against his own was making his blood sing and turning his mind to a puddle of goo.

Drake straightened and stripped Roman, his expression feverish and his movements jerky. Roman's cock throbbed when Drake disposed of his own clothes.

Fuck.

Drake's body was all hard angles and strong, toned muscles. His erection rose thickly from a nest of dark, trimmed pubes, the flushed, veiny surface glistening alluringly and the heavy balls beneath resting snugly against his thighs.

"Like what you see?" Drake said gruffly.

Roman nodded wordlessly, lust a living thing consuming him.

"Good." Drake raked Roman's naked form with his hot gaze. "I like what I see too. Very much so."

Drake took Roman's lips with his mouth and ran his hands possessively over Roman, exploring his hot flesh and quivering skin.

"Ah!"

Roman arched his back when Drake stroked his trembling cock with strong fingers. He parted his legs and bent his knees, inviting Drake into the cradle of his body.

"More!" Roman pleaded, not caring how needy he sounded.

Drake's eyes scorched him where he hovered above him. He let go of Roman's mouth and rained torrid kisses down Roman's neck and chest as he settled between Roman's thighs. By the time he worked his way down Roman's abs and took Roman's cock in his mouth, Roman was a whimpering mess.

Drake pressed Roman's knees wide open and went to town on Roman's erection, his tongue and lips working Roman's turgid flesh thoroughly, his stubble scraping the delicate skin of Roman's inner thighs. Roman fisted his hands in the pillow under his head and undulated wildly on the bed, his moans echoing around the bedroom as he drove his dick in and out of Drake's demanding mouth.

His climax stormed through him in a dizzying rush of blood and he came on a wild shout, his dick throbbing with pleasure so fierce it was almost pain.

Drake grunted and swallowed his cum hungrily.

Roman's ears buzzed when he collapsed on the bed a moment later, his skin coated with sweat. Drake rose on his knees between Roman's thighs. He fixed Roman with his scalding gaze and started rubbing his erection.

Roman licked his lips as he eyed Drake's thick shaft. "Let me."

Drake hissed when Roman scrambled onto his

knees and took hold of Drake's twitching length. Roman explored Drake's shape with his hands and teased the hot surface with tantalizing brushes of his lips and tongue, wrenching a curse from Drake.

Drake's hand found the back of Roman's head. He twisted his fingers in Roman's hair in a demanding grip and tugged Roman's mouth open.

"Suck me," he ordered gruffly, his cheeks stained with color.

Roman shivered at the command and did exactly that. He breathed carefully through his nose as he worked Drake's meaty cock through his lips. His cheeks and jaws bulged with delicious tension as Drake filled and stretched him.

"*Shit!*" Drake dropped his head back. "Your mouth is so fucking hot!"

He gave in to desire and punched his hips.

Roman grunted when Drake's erection dragged across his tongue and hit the back of his throat. He gripped Drake's thighs and started blowing him slow and deep.

Harsh groans and gasps fell from Drake's lips as he cradled Roman's head and thrust his cock in and out of Roman's mouth, his touch firm yet gentle despite the passion storming through him.

Roman knew Drake was close to his orgasm when his balls contracted. He dropped a hand to the quivering sac and fondled and squeezed it.

Drake cursed and exploded, his hips jerking fitfully as he filled Roman's mouth with his seed. He carried on thrusting as he rode his pleasure and didn't stop until he'd emptied the last drop of his cum down Roman's throat.

Drake panted for breathless moments before withdrawing his oversensitive flesh from Roman's mouth with a low hiss. He pulled Roman up and kissed him, their wet cocks touching intimately.

"If I didn't have to start work at your place in an hour, I would so tie you to this bed and fuck you into tomorrow," Drake groaned against Roman's lips.

Roman shivered, his hole twitching at the image Drake painted so vividly with his words. "Maybe you could play hooky for a day?"

Drake took hold of Roman's ass and pressed their groins together, drawing a moan from Roman. "Lara and Gary will kill me if I do that. And they'll get suspicious if you're missing too." He grabbed Roman's hand and dragged him off the bed and into the bathroom. "Come on, let's get cleaned up and grab breakfast."

CHAPTER SIXTEEN

"Oh wow," Roman groaned. "This is the best croissant I've ever tasted!"

A vestige of lust shot through Drake as he watched Roman lick his lips and swallow.

Shit. Why is it everything he does is so goddamn sexy?!

Elijah's voice roused Drake from his illicit daydream.

"Thank you." The chef smiled as he placed a tray of freshly prepared pastries in a commercial oven. "I'm glad you like it."

Drake had decided to bring Roman to Elijah's place for breakfast. Considering Roman's reputation, he'd opted for slipping into the building through the back door and eating in the kitchen.

Elijah carried on working around them, his movements efficient as he mixed batter and filled trays with soon-to-be baked goods. He'd gotten used to Carter and the rest of the Terrible Seven dropping by for breakfast in the last year and enjoyed the impromptu morning visits.

The swing door to the shop squeaked open.

"Hi, Elijah," Sam said briskly. "I came in early to check our—*holy shit, it's Roman Campbell!*" She rocked back on her heels and pressed a hand to her mouth, her eyes round.

"Any louder and they would have heard you in L.A.," Drake drawled.

"Roman Campbell's in our kitchen!" Sam hissed at Elijah, pointing an accusing finger at Roman.

"I know," Elijah said, unfazed. "He's Drake's new client."

"Hi." Roman grinned and slowly waved a hand. "Sam, is it?"

Sam's eyes glazed over slightly. "Hmm, yeah. Hi."

The back door opened on a gust of cool wind.

Alex and Hunter strolled in.

"Hi, Elijah. Could we grab some croissants to—?" Alex stopped abruptly when he clocked Drake and Roman sitting at the counter.

"Oh." A saccharine grin lit Hunter's face as he peered at them over Alex's shoulder. "And what do we have here?"

Drake sighed. It was bad enough that he'd refused to answer everyone's questions last Saturday night at *The Watering Hole*. Judging from the light in Hunter's eyes, he'd already sussed out that something might have happened between him and Roman.

"What we have here is two men having breakfast."

Drake frowned. "A client and his contractor, to be precise. This is a business meeting."

Roman swallowed a smile, the twinkle in his mocha eyes telling Drake he was recalling the torrid nature of their "business" that morning.

"Really?" Hunter said, clearly unconvinced.

A knowing smile curved Alex's lips. "So, we were right. Something *is* going on between you two."

Elijah stared, his gaze swinging from Alex to Drake and Roman. "It is?"

"Oh yeah. You weren't at the bar last weekend." Alex's smile widened. "Roman stormed into *The Watering Hole* and dragged Drake out back. They were gone for a while and Drake looked flustered when he came back."

"You were flustered?" Roman asked Drake.

"So were you, remember?" Drake muttered.

For some reason, he couldn't help but feel that Roman was seriously enjoying this.

"You could literally taste the sexual chemistry between them," Hunter told Elijah wisely.

The chef arched an eyebrow. "Oh."

Roman gazed at Drake. "Apparently, your friends think we have sexual chemistry."

If it weren't for the fact that he wanted to shield Roman from said friends' unwanted attention, Drake would have kissed the rockstar's sassy mouth there and then.

"I think we should finish up and leave."

Roman grinned at Drake's gruff tone. He drank the

last of his coffee and climbed off the bar stool. "Thanks for breakfast, Elijah." He dipped his chin at Alex and Hunter. "I'm afraid duty calls, gentlemen."

"Make sure you use a lot of lube," Hunter teased as they headed out the back door.

"Yeah," Alex added. "Drake's got the biggest dick of all of us."

"You should know," Hunter said.

"Shut up," Alex snapped. "That was a long time ago. And I'm more than satisfied with Finn's dick, thank you very much."

Drake scowled.

Roman studied Drake curiously as they strolled to the Jeep. "Alex is your ex?"

"Yes. We went out briefly when we were teenagers." Drake glanced at Roman, wondering if the rockstar was jealous.

Roman looked pensive. "I like your friends," he finally said with a smile.

"Really?" Drake grumbled. "'Cause there are times when I wish I could trade the assholes."

THE REST OF THAT DAY PASSED IN A RUSH OF ACTIVITY.

To Roman's relief, neither Lara nor Gary questioned the fact that Drake and Roman turned up on site together. Drake made up a story about bumping into each other in town and left it at that. After getting to know Drake a little, Roman knew he valued his professional relationship with his team and didn't want his personal affairs to overshadow them.

Though his heart still felt raw from talking about Ashley last night, Roman was glad he'd spoken to Drake about his past. It had been a cathartic experience in more ways than one. He wondered what his twin sister would have made of Drake if she were still alive.

That thought made Roman's chest tighten with sweet sadness.

He smiled. *I bet she'd be falling for him too.*

Drake had his head electrician repair the generator and connect the RV to the mains. A land clearance company turned up at lunch time and trimmed back the overgrown bushes and trees around the property, while Drake and his men cleared the mansion of debris and Gary and his assistants took delivery of the materials they would need to start the renovation project.

"We'll have a landscaping firm take care of shaping up the garden and the grounds after the main building work is done," Lara told Roman as she got ready to leave for the day. She glanced at the RV. "You sure you're gonna be okay in there? I was worried about you last night, what with that storm and everything."

"Yeah, I'm fine. Besides, Drake doesn't live far from here. I'll call him if I have any problem."

Lara smiled faintly. "I'm glad you two patched things up. He's a great guy."

"Who's a great guy?" Drake said, coming up behind them.

Lara grimaced. "Don't tell him," she ordered Roman. "It'll only go to his head."

Drake arched an eyebrow arrogantly. "Oh. So you were talking about me?"

Lara sighed. "Goodbye, Drake." She started walking away, paused, and turned. "I won't be on site for the rest of this week. I'll call for an update."

Drake dipped his chin. "Sure thing."

Dusk was falling by the time Drake's men vacated the grounds. Drake hung back and watched them leave.

Roman hesitated where they stood on the porch as Gary's truck rumbled down the driveway. "Can I come over tonight?"

Drake smiled and pulled him close. "Why don't we make it Friday night? It'll be the weekend then."

Roman made a face. "You're really good at resisting temptation, aren't you?"

Drake tipped Roman's chin up with a knuckle and brushed his lips across Roman's mouth. "It's not that, sweet cheeks. You're not gonna be able to walk straight the next day if I fuck you all night."

Heat flooded Roman's cheeks at the promise in Drake's eyes.

"You're gonna fuck me all night?" he breathed.

Drake nipped at Roman's lower lip with his teeth, his eyes dark pools of passion. "I'm gonna make you scream so hard your voice will be hoarse."

Roman shivered. *Shit.*

"So, what *are* you doing tonight?"

A noise disturbed them before Drake could reply. Drake let go of Roman and stepped back, his arms falling by his sides. Roman felt suddenly bereft without them. Even though he knew Drake was being careful for his own good, he couldn't help the bitter burn of rejection that twisted his stomach.

A familiar silver Jaguar came up the driveway and rolled to a stop next to the RV.

CHAPTER SEVENTEEN

Everyone groaned when Tristan laid out his cards.

"Read it and weep, suckers," Tristan drawled.

"Wait," James ordered coolly.

All eyes turned to the band manager. He studied Tristan with a steady green gaze and spread his cards on the table.

Tristan stilled.

"Son of a bitch." Admiration dawned on Hunter's face. "He has a full house!"

Shocked roars erupted across Wyatt's kitchen.

"Is this the first time Tristan's lost by any chance?" Nathan muttered to Theo.

Theo grinned and took a sip of his beer. "Sure looks that way."

Roman looped an arm around James's shoulders where he sat beside his band manager, a satisfied smile stretching his mouth.

"I told you you could beat him."

Irritation shot through Drake at the casual way Roman touched James.

James grunted, oblivious to the green monster lurking its head inside Drake. "I would be more impressed if we were playing with real money instead of game tokens."

Tristan narrowed his eyes. "Not all of us are filthy rich."

Hunter glanced at Tristan, a hint of surprise flashing in his eyes. Tristan was the wealthiest mechanic this side of the San Bernardino Mountains.

Drake frowned faintly when he sensed the underlying electric tension between Tristan and James.

Do they know each other?

"What'd we miss?" Izzy said breezily as she walked into the kitchen with Carter in tow. They'd just put Maisie to bed in Izzy's room.

"James beat Tristan," Alex announced with a grin.

Izzy gaped. "No way!" She stared from Tristan to James and back again, her eyes round.

Elijah flushed when Carter took the seat next to him and pulled him onto his lap. "Carter, we're with company!" he hissed.

"I see your honeymoon period is still in full flow," Izzy said tartly.

Carter grinned. "It's never gonna end."

Groans echoed around the room while Elijah blushed fiercely and scowled at his unrepentant husband.

"Yeah, yeah, everyone's having sex," Izzy grumbled.

"Except for me and Tristan." She pursed her lips. "The jury's still out on Drake."

Drake smiled and wordlessly drank his beer.

James glanced from Roman to Drake, his eyes darkening with a trace of displeasure.

Though the band manager hadn't said anything with regards to finding Drake and Roman together when he'd turned up at the estate a couple of hours ago, Drake couldn't help but sense he would disapprove if he found out about Drake and Roman's arrangement.

Drake suppressed a frown.

It's not like it's any of his business. Roman is a grown man.

❦

ROMAN CAME OUT OF WYATT AND IZZY'S DOWNSTAIRS bathroom to find James lurking in the corridor.

"Oh, hey." He smiled and cocked a thumb at the ceiling. "There's a bathroom upstairs."

"Are you and Drake fucking?" A muscle jumped in James's cheek as he glared at Roman.

Roman sucked in air. "What?"

"I said, are you and Drake—?"

"I heard what you said the first time!" Roman snapped. He grabbed James by the arm and dragged him down the passage and inside Wyatt's den. "What the hell is wrong with you?!" he spat, whirling around to face his best friend.

James scowled. "I'm worried about you."

Roman made a frustrated sound and threw his arms in the air. "You're always worried about me! It doesn't mean I'm going to stop living my life just to make you happy, James!"

James clenched his jaw. "Drake being your contractor makes any kind of relationship between you a conflict of interest, Roman. He should know this!"

"What, are you my lawyer now?!" Roman hissed. "And FYI, I'm the one who wanted us to sleep together!"

James recoiled slightly, shock making his eyes flare. "So you *are* sleeping with him!"

"We've slept in the same bed, but we didn't have sex," Roman said between gritted teeth. "Not that it's any of your business!" He cursed inwardly at the hurt in James's eyes and drew a deep breath. "The lights went out at the estate during the storm last night. I was having a full-blown panic attack when Drake found me. He drove me to his place and took care of me."

James sucked in air. "Why didn't you call one of us?!"

Roman made a face. "My phone died."

James swore colorfully.

Roman sighed. "Look, I get it. I get that you're worried that I'll screw up again and make the band suffer because of my—"

"That's not why I'm worried about you, goddammit!"

Roman rocked back on his heels at the fury and frustration darkening James's face. A fraught silence fell between them.

Dread coiled through Roman and quickened his pulse.

"What's really going on, James? This isn't like you at all."

James stayed quiet for a moment. He finally blew out a sigh and raked his hair with a hand. "It's your dad, Roman. I heard from our lawyers today." His knuckles whitened as he met Roman's shocked stare. "He's out on probation."

A buzzing noise filled Roman's ears. His chest tightened and his belly clenched. He bent over, a rasp leaving his lips as he tried to draw breath into his lungs.

"Roman!" James took a step toward him.

"Roman?"

Roman looked up dazedly.

Drake was standing in the doorway. His blue eyes turned stormy when he registered Roman's terrified expression. He strode inside the room and grabbed James by the neckline of his shirt.

"What the hell did you do to him?!"

James wrapped a hand around Drake's wrist and tugged, anger twisting his own face. "I didn't *do* anything to him. I just gave him some bad news!"

Roman swallowed convulsively. "It's my dad. My dad's out of jail!"

Drake let go of James, stunned. "What?"

He brushed past James and embraced Roman.

Roman shuddered, Drake's warmth wrapping around him like a cocoon and lending him strength. "That's why James came over. To tell me about my dad."

Drake squeezed him tightly. "How is that possible?" he asked James stiffly over Roman's head, the animosity draining out of his voice. "I thought he was doing time for embezzlement."

James scowled. "He knows?" he asked Roman accusingly.

"I told him last night," Roman murmured, a note of defiance creeping into his voice.

"Fuck." James clenched and unclenched his fists. "The bastard got out on good behavior." He grimaced at Roman and Drake's expressions. "Yeah, I don't believe it either."

Drake's hands tightened on Roman's back.

"He doesn't know where Roman is, does he?"

James shook his head. "No. And he's banned from making any sort of contact with Roman or talking about Roman to the press." He paused. "But he might still try and get to him."

"Because of his money?" Drake said harshly.

"That. And—" James faltered.

"And because he thinks I'm his property," Roman finished in a haggard voice.

CHAPTER EIGHTEEN

D RAKE GRIPPED THE STEERING WHEEL WITH WHITE knuckles and glanced at Roman.

Roman stared blindly out of the Jeep's passenger window, his face pale. He hadn't said a word since they'd left Wyatt and Izzy's house.

Drake had insisted that Roman spend the night with him again.

James had reluctantly concurred.

"I'll talk to our lawyers first thing in the morning," the band manager had said before he'd climbed inside his car. "See if we can get some kind of additional restraining order against your dad." His face had softened slightly when he'd locked eyes with Roman. "We won't let him hurt you again."

Though Roman had nodded numbly, Drake had sensed he hadn't really taken in any of James's reassurances. His eyes had gone lifeless, just as they had done when Drake had found him in the dark the night before.

Drake pulled into his driveway and parked outside the front porch of his home in a spray of gravel. He got out, rounded the Jeep, and opened the passenger door.

Roman sat frozen, his expression devoid of emotion.

Drake carefully took his hand and clenched his jaw at his icy skin.

Roman didn't protest when Drake guided him inside the house and through to the ensuite bathroom in the master bedroom.

Drake stripped himself and Roman of their clothes and walked Roman into the shower. Roman startled when the hot spray struck his skin. He blinked and looked around dazedly as he finally registered his surroundings.

Drake took him in his arms. Roman came willingly, his own hands locking on Drake's back as if he never wanted to let go. They stood like that for a while, the water pounding their heads and bodies.

Roman finally stirred in Drake's hold. "Drake?"

"Yes?"

"Make love to me."

Drake stiffened and pulled away slightly. "I don't think that's such a great idea right now."

Roman's pupils turned to dark pools of despair beneath him. "I want you to make me forget."

Drake gritted his teeth and closed his eyes briefly. He didn't want their first time together to be tainted by fear and anger. But he couldn't refuse Roman either. Not when Roman was looking at him as if he were his only lifeline in the world.

"Okay."

Roman shuddered when Drake lowered his head and took his lips. He wrapped his arms around Drake's neck and clung to him.

Drake kissed Roman until he moaned and trembled. He lifted his mouth from Roman's and looked down at Roman's erection, his pulse racing and desire dampening his apprehension.

They were both hard, their dicks digging into each other's bellies.

Drake grabbed his bottle of body wash, poured a generous amount in his hand, and started lathering Roman's pretty cock.

"*Ah!*" Roman clutched Drake's shoulders and jutted his hips at Drake's tender ministrations. "That feels good!"

Drake danced his tongue across Roman's left ear and down his tattoo as he continued rubbing him. "Let's get you cleaned up so I can fuck that sweet hole of yours."

Roman bit his lip and nodded.

Drake washed Roman from his head to his toes, his hands caressing and kneading Roman's quivering flesh and skin, heightening both their lust. Roman hissed in pleasure when Drake parted his cleft and rubbed his pucker before shoving two fingers inside. His cock jerked, dripping precum on Drake's thigh.

Drake gnashed his teeth, turned Roman around, and crowded him against the shower wall, the remaining doubts that this was a bad idea fading from his mind. He and Roman having sex was always going to happen. And he fully intended to make the experience unforgettable for both of them, despite the dark circumstances that had precipitated it.

With that thought in mind, Drake lowered himself to his knees, spread Roman's butt cheeks, and tongued his opening hungrily, giving in to his desire to experience Roman's sinful taste.

"*Fuck!*" Roman shouted, rising on his tip toes.

He dropped a hand to his cock and started rubbing himself as Drake thoroughly rimmed and sucked his hole. It didn't take long for him to climax, his cries echoing around the bathroom as he convulsed and spurted cum onto the granite tiles.

Drake rose, positioned his erection against Roman's cleft, and rubbed the underside of his shaft up and down Roman's twitching entrance.

"I can't wait to get *this* inside you!" he growled in Roman's ear.

Roman moaned and shifted his body.

Drake cursed when the new angle brought the head of his dick flush against Roman's folds.

"Do it," Roman begged. "Fuck me, Drake!"

Drake prayed to all the Gods and held himself back by a sheer act of will as Roman danced his hole against his straining cock. He kissed Roman's nape and bit down gently before licking the faint marks he'd made in Roman's skin.

"We have a way to go before that, Roman."

Roman let out a frustrated sound.

Drake stepped back and washed himself briskly, his erection a painful reminder that he had yet to orgasm.

Roman turned and stared at him with a glazed expression, his chest heaving with his breaths. His gaze dropped to Drake's thick shaft. He worried his lip with his pretty, white teeth, his eyes dark with hunger.

Drake tugged Roman out of the shower and dried them both in record time. He dropped the towel on the floor and walked Roman backward to his bed, his lips locked on Roman's and his tongue down Roman's throat.

The way Roman whimpered and clung to Drake told him he wanted it all.

They tumbled onto the sheets, Drake pressing Roman into the mattress as he continued kissing him ravenously, eager to feel the whole of him. Roman arched and rubbed himself against Drake, silently begging for more.

Drake finally relented and turned his attention to Roman's body, his heart pounding against his ribs. All he wanted was to draw Roman onto his hands and knees and pound his hole with his cock.

Soon! I have to fuck him soon!

Roman shivered and twitched as Drake caressed and kissed every inch of him. He cursed when Drake played with his nipple ring, Drake tugging on the metal repeatedly with his teeth before letting go and laving Roman's throbbing nub with his tongue.

"Cock!" Roman gasped. "I want to suck your cock!" He started scooting down the bed.

"Wait." Drake grabbed a bottle of lube and a box of condoms from the bedside table and settled his head and upper body on a couple of pillows near the foot of the bed. "Come here."

Roman obeyed eagerly.

"Turn around and straddle me," Drake ordered.

The way Roman flushed told Drake he knew exactly what he intended. He climbed atop Drake, his erection straining.

Lust burned through Drake when the position brought Roman's ass and cock over his face. "Perfect." He punched his hips and nudged his own dick against Roman's mouth. "Now, suck me."

Roman opened his mouth and started swallowing Drake, head bobbing as he worked Drake's thick erection eagerly over his tongue.

Drake hissed, pleasure tightening his belly. He opened the lube, coated his fingers, and spread Roman's butt cheeks.

Roman groaned and gasped around Drake's dick as Drake rimmed him with his tongue before thrusting two fingers through his softened folds.

Drake closed his wet hand around Roman's cock and stroked him with a delicious twisting motion before angling his shaft downward and sucking him.

Roman shivered and writhed above Drake as Drake finger fucked his hole and ate his cock. He sucked and licked and kissed Drake's dick with increasing desperation as he chased his orgasm.

A moan of frustration left Roman when Drake removed his fingers from his ass and let go of his dripping dick. Drake bit his lip hard as he withdrew his erection from Roman's scalding mouth.

There was only one place he wanted to come right now. And that was inside Roman's body.

Drake sheathed his trembling cock with a condom, poured lube all over himself, and knelt behind Roman.

"Spread your legs and grab on to the headboard."

Roman looked at Drake over his shoulder, his face flushed with passion.

"Do it, Roman," Drake growled. He leaned down and punished Roman with a stinging bite on his ass cheek.

Roman's pupils dilated. He obeyed Drake's command, the position opening him wide and giving both of them more control over what was about to happen.

Drake clutched Roman's hips and guided his cock to Roman's pucker.

Roman dropped his head and moaned as Drake nudged the thick head of his erection against the damp folds of his entrance. Drake's breaths shuddered out of him as he carefully punched his hips in a slow roll and entered Roman.

They gasped and groaned as Drake's dick stretched Roman deliciously wide. Drake paused when he reached the tight ring of muscles inside Roman. He waited until Roman's passage spasmed open before drawing back and sliding home in a single, powerful thrust.

"*Oh God!*" Roman shouted, his insides clenching tightly around Drake. "*Yes!* Just like that!"

Lust brought a red haze to Drake's vision at Roman's filthy cry. He looked down to where he was buried full hilt inside Roman's hole and cursed at the intoxicating sight. He pulled back and pushed in with another powerful thrust, hissing at the way Roman's rim dragged prettily on his cock.

"Yes!" Roman sobbed, his hands fisting on the headboard and his back arching with pleasure. "That feel so good! Deeper! *Harder!*"

Drake finally gave Roman what he so desperately wanted and punched forward again and again, marveling at how tight and hot and hungry Roman's passage was. His balls slapped against Roman's ass as his movements grew more savage, harsh grunts falling from his lips.

Roman met Drake's thrusts with equally fierce motions of his body, driving his hole back and forth over the thick intruder impaling him, eager to give as much as he was receiving.

Drake's orgasm shivered down his spine and pooled in his lower belly. He bit his lip and groaned as he pistoned his aching cock in and out of Roman's hole, seeking the growing ball of pleasure.

Drake leaned forward and clasped Roman's right hand on the headboard, sweat dripping from his face and splashing onto Roman's undulating back.

Roman dropped a hand to his cock and started giving himself a brisk rub, his mouth open on untamed keens of pleasure. He soon stiffened and came on a guttural cry, his passage squeezing painfully around Drake's throbbing rod.

Drake's balls rose as he climaxed inside Roman, ecstasy causing stars to explode in front of his eyes. He shoved his spurting cock erratically in and out of Roman's quivering passage as waves of intense pleasure surged through him.

Roman moaned when Drake collapsed onto him a moment later, taking him down onto the sheets, his spent cock still buried in Roman's ass. They shuddered and panted, the dying pulses of their orgasms quivering through their bodies.

"Wow," Drake murmured against Roman's nape.

"That's my line," Roman mumbled.

Drake nuzzled Roman's flesh before pressing a kiss to his damp skin. "That was amazing. Was it good for you too?"

Roman groaned. "Do you even have to ask?" He shivered when Drake slowly pulled out of him.

Roman twisted on his side and watched Drake dispose of the used condom. Drake returned to bed and settled against the headboard before pulling Roman up so that Roman's back was flush against his chest.

"Want to take a breather and go again?"

"Hell yes!" Roman said.

Drake chuckled and nuzzled his hair, his heart light and his chest throbbing with an unnamed emotion.

CHAPTER NINETEEN

Light washed across Roman's eyelids in soft, warm waves. He stirred and slowly blinked his eyes open, his mind fuzzy and his body pleasantly sated.

Sunlight danced through the gauzy curtains fluttering at the window next to Drake's bed. Roman turned and stretched an arm out, seeking Drake.

The sheets next to him were cool.

He frowned, started to sit up, and froze.

"Fuck."

His lower body hurt like a bitch and the burn of penetration stung his back passage. Roman flushed as he recalled all the wicked things that had happened between him and Drake last night.

Drake had kept his promise and fucked him until the sky lightened and Roman was hoarse from shouting in pleasure.

That bastard's stamina is scary. Roman frowned. *Where is he, anyway?*

A sheet of folded paper on the bedside table caught his eyes. Roman carefully leaned over and took it.

It was a note from Drake.

I've gone to your place. Breakfast is in the oven. Draw yourself a bath and relax for the day. I'll be back tonight. Drake.

A wry smile tilted Roman's lips. The man he was falling in love with was not one for pretty words.

He stilled in the next instant, his eyes widening.

Whoa, where did that come from?!

Roman stared blindly at the note, his pulse quickening.

Am I—am I really falling in love with Drake?

He only had to feel the clenching in his chest and belly to know the answer.

Well, shit.

Roman worried his lip for a moment, equally thrilled and anxious at the new feelings swirling through him. Drake had made it clear that this was just a fling for him. As for Roman, he'd never intended to fall for the man. He sighed and raked his mussed-up hair with a hand.

Life really has a way of throwing wrenches in my plans.

Roman decided worrying about his burgeoning love for Drake wasn't going to solve anything and made his way to the bathroom, wincing and cursing Drake under his breath. An hour-long hot bath soothed most of his aches and he felt refreshed by the time he dressed in the clean clothes Drake had left him and headed into the kitchen.

Roman took the croissants Drake had prepared for

him, made a coffee, and headed out onto the deck overlooking the rear yard. Though it was slightly chilly, the stillness of Drake's home and the sounds of the forest acted like a much-needed balm on his soul.

He was still upset about his dad being out of jail. Roman realized that there wasn't a lot he could do about it. Like his therapist had told him repeatedly in rehab, there was only so much he could control. The one thing he would always have power over was how he chose to respond to anything that threatened the life he'd made for himself.

As he sat staring at the trees and the branches swaying the bright sky, the deep-seated fear that had lived inside Roman for most of his life and that had reared its ugly head last night slowly turned to anger.

Neither he nor Ashley were to blame for their father's horrific behavior. And neither was their mom, even though Roman suspected he would never forgive her for abandoning them.

Roman's dad was a monster, plain and simple. And monsters needed to be conquered.

His eyes widened. He grabbed his cell and brought up the song he'd been working on, eager to pen the new lyrics that had just come to his mind.

Roman spent the rest of the day in front of the fire Drake had left burning in the hearth, the words pouring out of him as if a dam had burst open in his heart. He wrote until his fingers ached, his heart racing with excitement as he hummed potential tunes for the lyrics.

He couldn't wait to show these songs to James and the band.

Dusk was falling when Roman finally stirred and saw the time.

He should be home soon.

⁂

DRAKE TOOK OFF HIS HARD HAT, WIPED THE SWEAT FROM his brow, and studied the mansion hallway with a contented feeling.

They'd made a lot of headway today and the place was starting to take on the shape of Lara and Roman's designs.

"Jeez, if you keep working me and the boys this hard, we're gonna need a holiday by the time we finish this project," Gary drawled as he came up beside him.

Drake grimaced at his foreman.

"Sorry. I'm just really excited about this place."

"I can tell," Gary murmured with a smile.

Drake couldn't tell the foreman the other reason he'd worked them so hard today. The physical effort had helped take Drake's mind off the alluring man he'd left in his bed that morning and the vivid memories of last night.

Sex with Roman had been mind blowing in more ways than one and Drake couldn't recall being this physically satisfied in a long time.

Which made the hunger still simmering inside him all the more baffling.

He'd thought his desire for Roman would abate

somewhat after they made love. Instead, the lust burning through Drake's veins for the man who had surrendered his body so willingly to him last night seemed to have intensified.

The only time he'd felt a semblance of a similar passion was when he'd been with Alex. The face of his former lover danced before Drake's eyes. To his surprise, he didn't experience the tug in his belly that indicated he still held lingering feelings for the lawyer.

Drake was musing over this development as he walked to his Jeep, when his cell phone rang. He stopped with his keys in hand, saw the name on the screen, and took the call.

"Hi, Izzy. What's up?"

"Drake?" Izzy's voice trembled at the other end of the line.

Drake stiffened. "What's wrong?"

"You need to come to the care home," Izzy mumbled, her words choked with tears. "It's—it's Miles!"

Drake went weak at the knees, the keys dropping from his hand. He leaned a hand on the hood of the Jeep, fear knotting his stomach as half a dozen scenarios played across his mind, each as terrible as the other.

"What happened to Miles?! Is he—?!"

"He's awake, Drake," Izzy sobbed. "Miles is awake!"

CHAPTER TWENTY

A SOUND WOKE ROMAN. HE LIFTED HIS HEAD AND realized he'd fallen asleep on Drake's couch. He sat up groggily and glanced at his watch.

It was past 2 a.m.

The fire had died down and the only illumination came from the soft lights of the standing lamps dotting the open plan floor space.

"Drake, is that you?" Roman called out, anxiety overcoming the irritation that had plagued him all evening.

Drake appeared from the direction of the hallway. "You're still up?"

Roman's anger faded when he registered Drake's distracted expression.

"What's wrong?"

"I'm sorry, I didn't see your messages until just now. I should have called you." Drake came over and sat down heavily beside Roman. He leaned his head back and closed his eyes, his face haggard.

"Drake, you're scaring me," Roman said worriedly.

Drake opened his eyes and clasped Roman's hand. "Sorry, I didn't mean to—"

"Stop saying you're sorry and tell me what's going on!" Roman snapped.

Drake's fingers twitched on Roman's skin. He clenched his jaw.

"It's Miles. Miles woke up."

Shock reverberated through Roman. "What?!"

Drake swallowed and linked his fingers with Roman. "Izzy called just as I was leaving your place. She was at the care home with Miles's mom. Miles just opened his eyes and—" He stopped, his face flushing with emotion.

Roman took Drake in his arms, his heart thundering against his ribs. He couldn't imagine what Drake was going through right now. Drake welcomed his embrace with a shaky inhale and clung to him fiercely.

"Did the others—" Roman started.

Drake nodded against Roman's neck. "Izzy got all of us. We've been there the whole evening."

Roman stroked Drake's back with soothing motions as he shuddered against him. "Is Miles okay?"

"Yeah." Drake pulled back and stared at Roman, his eyes glistening. "He's absolutely fine. It's like the last twelve years never happened." A low chuckle left him then.

"What?" Roman said, puzzled.

"He called us old men."

A faint smile curved Roman's lips. "I hope you

didn't remind him he was the same age as the rest of you."

"Hunter almost did, but Tristan stepped on his foot and Izzy elbowed him in the ribs." Drake's face grew serious. "I'm sorry. I knew you were waiting for me, but I was so caught up in—"

"Shh." Roman pressed a finger against Drake's mouth. "Stop apologizing. I'm just glad you're okay."

"I'm more than okay." Drake took Roman in his arms. "I still can't believe he's with us again. I mean, he's always been with us, but he's…back. Miles is back and it feels like a part of me that I didn't even know was missing has returned to me."

Roman's belly twisted as he listened to Drake's trembling voice. It was his first time seeing Drake so vulnerable. It only affirmed his growing feelings for the man. Roman could no longer deny the truth.

He was completely, madly, and utterly in love with Drake Jackson.

Drake pressed a kiss to Roman's hair, oblivious to the gut-wrenching realization storming through Roman. "Will you come with me when I go visit tomorrow afternoon? I'll ask Gary to cover for me at the construction site."

Roman startled, more than a little surprised. "Are you sure?"

"Yes." Drake smiled. "I want you to meet Miles."

Roman hesitated before nodding. "Okay."

Drake saw the pile of papers Roman had spent the day scribbling on and lifted the top sheet. "Is this what you were working on today?"

Roman settled against Drake and nodded. "Yeah. It's the songs for our next album."

Drake's eyes widened as he studied the lyrics. "This is nice."

Roman's ears grew hot. "Thanks."

"So, what else did you do?" Drake wrapped an arm around Roman's shoulders and tucked him against his side.

"I ate the croissants you made for me. And I spent some time sitting out on the deck." Roman paused, his cheeks warming as he glanced sideways at Drake. "And I took that bath you suggested."

Drake grimaced. "Is your body okay?"

Roman bit his lip and nodded.

"Good." Drake sighed and kissed the tip of Roman's nose. "I was worried I'd been too hard on you last night."

"You were hard alright," Roman mumbled.

Drake made a face. "Jokes? Really?"

"Hey, I'm not the one who opened that can of worms," Roman protested.

Drake chuckled. The laughter slowly faded from his face as the air between them thickened with sexual tension.

"Drake," Roman breathed.

Drake made a sound at the back of his throat, curled a hand on Roman's jawline, and took his lips in a demanding kiss.

A tremulous sigh washed out of Roman as he twisted and looped his arms languidly around Drake's neck, eagerly welcoming Drake's tongue inside his mouth. He gasped when Drake took hold of his waist and maneuvered him onto his lap.

They both cursed as their erections touched tantalizingly through the material of their pants. Drake shrugged Roman's shirt over his head and dropped it on the floor, the same urgency quickening Roman's pulse evident in his darkening eyes. Roman flushed as Drake stared at him heatedly, his gaze scorching Roman's skin everywhere it landed.

"You're so beautiful," Drake whispered reverently. He kissed and stroked Roman's face and neck and chest, his fingers and lips dancing achingly over Roman's flesh.

Roman drowned in Drake's touch, hips undulating above Drake's groin as he rubbed their straining cocks together. The sweet friction made his belly clench and his hole twitch in anticipation.

Drake pulled and twisted Roman's right nipple between his thumb and forefinger while he kissed and yanked on Roman's left nipple ring with his teeth, drawing hisses of pleasure-pain from Roman's throat as he stretched the nub deliciously taut.

Roman shivered when Drake caressed his abs and teased his fingers along the deep V leading to his crotch.

Drake stripped Roman of his jeans and boxers before taking care of his own clothes, his chest heaving with his breaths and desire painting red stains on his cheekbones. Roman shuddered when Drake positioned him on his lap once more and pulled him to his knees, his hands fondling and kneading Roman's butt cheeks.

Roman grasped the headrest and clung on for dear life as Drake rained kisses along the path his fingers had taken, his face close to Roman's straining erection.

CHAPTER TWENTY-ONE

"Drake," Roman moaned.

"Tell me," Drake murmured, his eyes dark with lust as he gazed up at Roman. "Tell me what you want me to do to you, Roman."

"*Ah!*" Roman jerked as Drake grazed his sensitive shaft with his knuckles.

"What do you want, Roman?" Drake growled, fingers dipping inside Roman's cleft, pulling him wide and exposing his hole.

"I want you to suck my cock!" Roman gasped, his pucker twitching. "I want you to fuck me. I want you to make me come over and—*Ahhhh! Yes! Oh God! Just like that!*"

Roman's voice faded to a low moan as Drake swallowed his aching cock all the way to the back of his throat. The wicked sounds their flesh made as Drake started blowing him slow and deep had Roman's knuckles whitening on the headrest.

Roman dropped his head forward, pleasure

washing over him in dizzying waves. He started to roll his hips, driving his dick repeatedly through Drake's scalding lips and along his clever tongue, his orgasm a tight ball growing inside his belly.

Drake coated his fingers with Roman's precum and teased Roman's hungry opening. Roman whimpered at the dual stimulation, his folds contracting under Drake's touch. Drake slipped two fingers inside Roman, searched for his prostate, and massaged the firm bump.

"*Oh fuck!*" Roman cried out.

He curled his toes, pleasure arrowing through him like a lightning bolt.

Drake repeated the movement over and over again, his breaths heavy as he sucked Roman's cock with powerful motions of his jaw.

A buzzing noise filled Roman's ears. His vision flickered when he finally exploded on a guttural shout, his nails digging into the leather and his passage clenching fiercely on Drake's fingers as he climaxed.

"Drake! Drake!"

Roman chanted Drake's name over and over again as he convulsed, his throbbing cock filling Drake's throat with his cum.

Drake waited until Roman collapsed against him before letting go of his sensitive dick and withdrawing his fingers from his body. He lowered Roman to his lap, nipped at the pulse thrumming at the base of Roman's throat, and started to shift Roman off him.

"I need to grab a condom."

"Don't." Roman lifted his head and met Drake's

startled gaze, his heart thumping in his chest. "I want you to fuck me without one."

Drake stilled. "What?"

Roman swallowed, more than a little shocked at his own suggestion. "I'm clean, if that's what you're worried—"

Drake shook his head, his eyes gunmetal blue pools of desire. "That's not what I'm worried about. And I'm clean too." He faltered. "Have you ever done it bareback before?"

Roman shook his head. "No. You?"

"Once."

Roman couldn't help the stab of jealousy that pierced his chest.

"Was it Alex?"

Drake nodded. "Yeah. It was only the one time."

Roman looked down at Drake's erection and ran a knuckle lightly up and down his twitching shaft.

Drake cursed.

"I want to feel you," Roman breathed. "All of you. Bare."

Drake shuddered and closed his eyes briefly. He leaned around Roman, grabbed his wallet from his pants, and removed a packet of lube from inside.

Roman's pulse thundered in his veins as he watched Drake tear the foil with his teeth and empty the content in one hand. Drake stroked his cock while Roman stared avidly, his breaths ragged and his pupils dark with hunger as he made himself nice and slick.

Roman gasped when Drake turned his attention to his hole. He clutched the back of the couch with one hand, spread his thighs wide, and grabbed his right butt cheek, stretching himself open for Drake.

Drake growled in approval and started plundering his passage with two fingers, thrusting and twisting before scissoring them.

"*Ah!*" Roman shuddered and arched when Drake pushed a third finger inside him.

Drake kissed Roman's throat and bit down on his collarbone as he worked Roman's hole deliciously open. He yanked his fingers out of Roman's ass a moment later, gripped Roman's hips, and positioned him above his thick rod.

"Oh!" Roman gasped as Drake nudged his pucker with the broad head of his bare cock. He looked down and almost came at the sight of Drake's dick about to enter him. "*Yes!*"

Drake cursed when Roman grabbed his straining shaft and bore down on him. They both groaned when Drake's dick parted Roman's sweet folds and slipped inside an inch.

"Shit!" Drake growled against Roman's throat. He swallowed heavily. "You're so hot and tight! You feel *fucking* amazing!"

Roman panted and forced his body to relax as he took another inch of Drake's erection. He stilled when Drake reached the tight ring guarding his inner passage.

Drake took his mouth in a passionate kiss and thrust up gently.

Roman moaned as the band of muscles stretched to accommodate Drake's thick cock, the sting and burn dancing through his passage. Then Drake was all the way inside and Roman lost his fucking mind.

"Oh God!" Roman whimpered brokenly, his insides so full and tight he didn't know where he ended and Drake began. There was only thing he was certain of in that raw moment of intimacy.

He was never going to get enough of the dirty feeling of taking Drake bareback.

"You're so big!" Roman moaned. "Your cock feels *so* good! Fuck me, Drake!'

Drake made an animal sound, fixed Roman's waist in a punishing grip, and started punching his hips in deep, powerful thrusts. Stars exploded in front of Roman's eyes as Drake's dick nudged the soft bump of his prostate.

Roman's cock jerked and spurted out precum as he grabbed the back of the couch. He rose and fell on Drake's thick rod, his folds kissing the hot, veiny surface with every drag of his taut rim on Drake's aching flesh.

"Ah! *Oh!* Oh God! *Yes! Yes!*"

Roman lost track of time as he rode Drake, their movements as savage as they were passionate. He came once, twice, three times. And still Drake fucked him, wrenching cry after cry from Roman's throat.

Drake's breath stuttered and his thrusts grew erratic as he finally neared his climax. He bit Roman's shoulder and came on an animal grunt, his cock pulsing deep inside Roman. Roman's belly trembled as Drake's hot cum filled his insides. He clenched his passage at the filthy feeling and drew a curse from Drake.

Their harsh pants echoed in the silence when they finally came down from their highs, their bodies limp where they'd collapsed against one another.

"That was—" Drake started.

"The best sex I've ever had," Roman mumbled.

Drake lifted his head and stared at Roman, looking more than a little pleased. "Really?"

Roman nodded. "Hands down. The. Best. Sex. I've never—"

Drake swallowed the rest of Roman's words in a kiss that made his heart tremble.

"Same," he whispered against Roman's lips, his eyes glittering with emotion. "Now, how about I clean you up before we do that all over again?"

Roman flushed and bit his lip when Drake carefully lifted him off his spent cock, his passage throbbing at the sudden empty feeling. He sucked in air when Drake's cum oozed out of his hole and down the inside of his thighs, his eyes widening at the new sensation.

A husky moan fell from Roman's lips when Drake reached between his legs and fingered the sticky mess he'd made of him.

"Fuck." Drake's eyes burned with fresh hunger as he took Roman's hand and dragged him to the bedroom.

CHAPTER TWENTY-TWO

THE SUNSHINE CARE HOME WAS LOCATED IN A secluded valley, in the mountains to the north of Twilight Falls.

Roman stared at the pretty, two-story, red-shingle roof building when it came into view through the sunlit trees beneath them. They'd passed the sign for the care home a while ago, after turning into a side road. He spotted an immaculate garden with shrubs and rockery surrounding the building where it sat on a rise that spilled gently toward Twilight Falls River.

Drake took the last bend in the winding road, headed down a driveway, and pulled up in a bay reserved for motorcycles. He studied the black and red classic Triumph motorcycle and the bevy of vehicles in the parking lot as he took off his helmet.

"Looks like the whole gang's already here."

"Are you sure this is okay?" Roman removed his helmet and climbed off the motorcycle from where he'd been riding on the back.

Drake sighed. "Stop being such a worry wart."

He led Roman up the path leading to the front porch and ushered him inside a brightly-lit reception.

The brunette behind the desk looked up from her computer and did a comical double take.

"Holy Jesus Fuck, it's Roman Campbell," she announced in a leaden voice.

Roman frowned at Drake. "Told you this was a bad idea."

"Don't worry." A grim half-smile tilted Drake's lips. "The care home policy states that its employees can't divulge the identity of its visitors, however famous they may be. Isn't that right, Lisa?"

Lisa narrowed her eyes. "Is that a threat, Jackson?"

Drake arched an eyebrow. "If I wanted to threaten you, I'd tell the world what you did when you were in fifth grade, in Mrs. Lany's class. You know, when you—"

Lisa jumped to her feet and raised a hand in a conciliatory gesture.

"Whoa, whoa, whoa! Steady there, Tiger! No need to go for the jugular."

Roman bit back a smile. He could tell Drake and Lisa were friends from the way they teased each other.

"Now, how about you show us the visitor's log and we sign in?" Drake said.

Lisa grumbled something under her breath and gave them the book.

She stared at the name Roman wrote down. "Yogi Bear?"

Roman flashed her a smile that made her blink. "He's a cool bear."

Lisa chewed her lower lip before directing a shrewd stare at Drake.

"Please tell me you guys are fucking? That mental imagery could keep me going for months."

Roman gaped, too shocked to speak.

"Ignore her," Drake growled. "She's a hard-core gay romance fan and has fantasies about anyone with a dick."

Lisa grinned, unrepentant. "He's on the porch out back."

Apprehension knotted Roman's stomach as Drake led him through the sprawling building and onto a terrace overlooking the rear garden and the river. Though Drake didn't seem to think much of bringing him here, the move meant a hell of a lot to Roman.

Drake was letting him into a part of his life he held dear. And that gave Roman hope. That Drake wanted this thing between them to be more than just a fling.

Izzy's laughter reached them as they turned the corner of the building. Roman slowed, feeling somewhat awkward as they approached the group gathered around a man in a wheelchair.

Miles Martinez was handsome in the kind of way that reminded Roman of the Hollywood actors who'd graced the movie screens in the 1970s. His dark hair curled slightly at his nape and dimples dotted his cheeks when he smiled at something Izzy said. He looked to be about as tall as Hunter and Alex and had a slender build that only added to his air of fragility.

Roman recalled what Drake had told him that morning.

Even though Miles had been unconscious for twelve years, the care he'd received meant his muscles hadn't wasted like most coma patients. He had physical therapy every day, most of it provided by the care home and the rest paid for by his mother. The insurance money Miles and Elaine Martinez had received after the accident meant Miles's needs would be taken care of for the rest of his life. He wouldn't even need to work if he chose not to.

The rest of the Terrible Seven and their relevant other halves were sprawled out on the floor and the deck chairs around Miles. An elderly woman with Miles's eyes and gray peppered hair sat next to Miles, her gnarly hand clasped firmly in his.

Miles brightened when he saw Drake. "Hey, Drake."

"Hey." Drake went over and hugged Miles, his eyes darkening with emotion.

Miles looked past him to Roman, his gaze curious. "Who's this?"

"Oh my." Elaine Martinez pressed a hand to her chest and stared at Roman. "You are that famous rockstar."

Hunter's eyes rounded. "You listen to Crazyknot, Elaine?!"

"I heard them on the radio and bought one of their albums." Elaine sniffed at their disbelieving looks. "I played it for Miles. Besides, an old lady can still enjoy rock 'n' roll."

Roman smiled. He liked Elaine Martinez already.

"You're a rockstar?" Miles said hoarsely, his awed expression so similar to his mother's Roman had to bite his lip. "Like, Nickelback?"

Everyone stared at Miles.

"What?" he said slightly defensive. "They were popular the year I had the accident."

Roman burst out laughing, unable to suppress his mirth at the range of pitying expressions that dawned on the faces of the people around Miles.

WARMTH BLOSSOMED INSIDE DRAKE AT ROMAN'S carefree laughter.

The rockstar looked more relaxed than he'd appeared when he first got here.

Even Drake had had second thoughts about his suggestion that Roman come with him today when he'd woken up late that morning. One look at Roman's face where he slept tucked up against Drake had convinced him it had been the right decision to make.

Drake wasn't quite ready to explore the exact reasons why he wanted Roman to be a welcomed member of the circle of friends he held so dear to his heart. All he knew was that he wanted Roman to be a part of his life, more than just as a lover.

It was Alex who grilled him a couple of hours later, when they went in to get refreshments for the others.

"So, what's going on between you and Roman?"

Drake stiffened slightly before meeting his former lover's stare over the coffee machine.

"What makes you think there's something going on between us?"

"Oh, please," Alex scoffed. "The sexual chemistry between you guys is off the charts."

Drake cursed internally.

Alex had always been perceptive about stuff like that.

"So, the two of you are dating?" Alex asked insistently.

Drake sighed. It was clear he wasn't going to get away without giving his friend an answer.

"It's a temporary arrangement."

Lines wrinkled Alex's brow. "What do you mean?"

"Roman wanted a fuck buddy while he was in Twilight Falls." Drake shrugged, hoping his nonchalant tone would be enough to deter Alex. "I obliged."

Alex's frown deepened. "So, you're saying you guys are sex friends?"

Drake lowered his gaze and concentrated on making their drinks. "Yes."

"That's bullshit."

Drake's hands stilled. He scowled at Alex. "What the hell is your problem?"

Alex poked Drake's chest with a finger. "My problem is that I can see you making the same mistake you made with me. And FYI, sex friends don't do the kind of shit you've done with Roman."

Drake's stomach twisted at the anger blazing in Alex's eyes.

"They don't bring their fuck buddy over for a game

of poker," Alex continued. "And they definitely don't drag them along to visit a sick friend."

"Is everything okay?" someone said behind them.

Drake whirled around.

Roman stood a few feet away, a guarded expression on his face.

"Yeah." Drake directed a warning glance at Alex. "Everything's fine."

Alex took one of the trays and twisted on his heels. He stopped by Roman.

"I get the feeling this guy might treat you like a jackass at some point in the future," he told the rockstar in clipped tones. "I'm here if you want to talk." He flashed a frown at Drake and disappeared in the direction of the terrace.

CHAPTER TWENTY-THREE

"Can you drop me off at my place?" Roman said.

Drake studied Roman with a frown as they stopped next to the motorcycle. "Are you sure you want to do that? We don't know your father's whereabouts yet."

"I can't stay at your house forever."

Drake hesitated. "Look, I'm sorry about what Alex said. He doesn't—"

"It's okay." Roman smiled thinly. "We both agreed this was going to be a temporary arrangement." He turned and climbed on the back of Drake's Harley, his heart aching.

The argument Roman had overheard between Drake and Alex echoed through his mind as he clung to Drake on the ride into town. He knew what Drake had said was the truth. Still, he'd hoped Drake had come to share some of the feelings that had been growing inside him over the past few days. Feelings Roman never meant to have but were now irrevocably embedded in his heart and soul.

A bitter smile twisted his lips.

Who would have thought the great Roman Campbell would get rejected by his very first love?

Roman suspected something else lay behind Drake's fear of falling in love. From what he'd heard Alex say, it appeared the reason he and Drake had broken up was because Drake had been unwilling to commit to him.

They reached the mansion far too soon for Roman's liking. Drake pulled up next to the RV and turned off the Harley's engine. Silence fell between them as Roman climbed off and handed his helmet to Drake, the dying sunlight filtering through the trees and dappling them in light and shadow.

"Have dinner with me tonight," Drake said gruffly.

Roman hesitated. Part of him wanted to say no. But the other part still hungered for Drake's touch. He swallowed a sigh.

There was no point lingering on something beyond his control. He couldn't force Drake to fall in love with him. But he could enjoy his company and his body while their arrangement lasted.

"Okay," Roman murmured. "I still have my stuff to pick up from your place anyway."

"I'll come get you in an hour." Drake curled his fingers around Roman's nape and pulled him in for a passionate kiss.

Roman gasped and clutched Drake's shoulders. Desire surged through his veins instantly, as if Drake had flipped a switch inside him. The promise in Drake's eyes when he let him go made Roman's belly clench. He watched Drake's motorcycle disappear down the driveway and cursed his half-hard cock as he headed inside the motorhome.

Roman tidied the place and caught up with James and Kurt to distract himself. His best friend and the Crazyknot lead guitarist got excited when they heard about the new songs he'd written.

"I'll send them to you tomorrow," Roman promised, gathering his dirty clothes.

"Why not tonight?" Kurt groaned. "Come on, man. You know I hate waiting!"

"I've got plans tonight."

"Oh?" Kurt raised his eyebrows on the video call. "What kind of plans?"

"I'm having dinner with a friend," Roman said evasively.

James frowned. "You mean, you're having sex with Drake."

Kurt sucked in air. "Wait. Who's Drake?!"

Roman narrowed his eyes and put his laundry in the wash.

"Drake is none of your business. I'm hanging up."

"Hey, don't be like that," Kurt protested. He grinned. "So, this Drake? Is he packing a big—"

Roman disconnected with a scowl.

A noise outside reached his ears just as he was about to turn the washing machine on. He glanced at the time.

He's early.

Roman straightened, went over to the door, and opened it. "Hey, I wasn't expecting you for another—"

The rest of his words died in his throat.

A sneer twisted Dusty Leyman's face as he stared at him. "Hello, son."

Roman's stomach dropped, terror drenching him in a cold sweat.

***

DRAKE FINISHED MARINATING THE STEAKS, PLACED THEM in the fridge, and headed out of his house.

He'd topped up on lube and condoms at a pharmacy after he'd dropped Roman off at the Strickland Estate and changed the bedding in his room. A determined frown wrinkled his brow as he started the Harley and headed out onto the road.

Drake had every intention of getting those sheets nice and filthy with Roman later. He suspected Roman was still upset about the argument he'd overheard between him and Alex and he intended to make him forget about it, at least for tonight and into the weekend.

He'd hesitated briefly when he'd bought the condoms. He wanted to give Roman the choice of using them, even though it would dash Drake's hopes if he did. Bareback sex with Roman was out of this world and Drake couldn't get enough of it.

Drake's headlight lit up Roman's driveway when he rode up the incline minutes later. The RV appeared around the bend.

The door was open and the lights were on.

Drake parked the Harley, climbed off, and headed inside the motorhome.

"Roman, are you ready?"

Silence greeted him. The RV was empty.

Drake frowned. The lock light on the washing machine was blinking. He exited the motorhome and looked around the grounds of the estate, puzzled.

Where is he?

A faint shout reached him. His gaze swung to the mansion.

Drake was up the steps and inside the building in seconds, his pulse racing with dread. Fear knotted his stomach when he saw Roman's smashed up phone in the hallway. He bolted toward the sound of the raised voices coming from the rear of the house, his heart in his throat.

Drake rocked to a stop when he entered the kitchen.

Roman stood braced on the other side of the old granite island that dominated the room. He was holding a chair above his head and glaring at the middle-aged man who faced him.

"Get away from me, you asshole!"

He threw the chair and backed away, his frantic gaze searching for another weapon as it smashed into the man.

The guy cursed and straightened from his half crouch. "You little shit! That hurt!" His eyes narrowed to dark pools of hatred as he dusted splinters from his clothes. "You seemed to have grown a spine since the last time I saw you, you faggot. Come here! Daddy needs to teach you a lesson." He started toward Roman.

Drake stormed across the floor, grabbed the man's

arm, and sent him crashing into the pantry door. He walked over to Roman and gently cradled his face with one hand.

"Are you okay?" Drake growled, his gaze searching Roman's face and body for injuries. "Did he touch you?!"

Roman shook his head, his eyes shifting briefly from the figure rising off the floor on the other side of the room to lock with Drake's. "No." Defiance and outrage eclipsed the fear in the mocha depths. "I didn't let him get close enough."

Relief made Drake dizzy. He gritted his teeth and scowled at Roman's attacker. "I take it this man's your father?"

The stranger spoke before Roman could reply.

"Are you fucking this guy?" The anger darkening the man's face faded, only to be replaced by a sneer of pure contempt. "I guess you're like your mom, after all. Ready to spread your legs for anything with a dick—"

Drake moved, a red veil of rage filling his vision. He grabbed Roman's father by his shoulder and punched him in the face. The guy grunted and staggered back, blood spurting from his broken nose.

Drake slipped his cell phone out of his jeans and lobed it at Roman. "Call the cops. I'll hold him off." He turned and narrowed his eyes at Roman's father. "Now, how about I teach you a little respect while we wait for them to get here."

CHAPTER TWENTY-FOUR

"I can't believe you beat the crap out of the guy," Tristan muttered as they came out of the police station. "I'll be surprised if he doesn't press charges."

"He violated the terms of his probation and attacked Roman," Drake snarled. "That asshole doesn't have a leg to stand on!"

Roman half-listened to their words, his anxious gaze on Drake.

"Is your hand okay?"

Drake nodded, his face softening. "It's nothing time won't heal." He clenched and unclenched his bruised right fist.

It was past 10 p.m. and they'd just finished giving their statements to a couple of Twilight Falls police officers. A rumble of excitement had raced through the station when the men and women who worked there realized Roman had been involved in the assault that had been reported to 911 earlier that evening. Twilight Falls didn't exactly have a high crime rate and a juicy incident centered around a world famous rockstar had gripped their attention like little else could.

To Roman's relief, the sheriff had gotten on top of his officers' rabid curiosity with a few stern words about confidentiality and what he would personally do to them if he found out they'd blabbed to the press about the disturbance at the Strickland Estate.

Tristan glanced at Drake's swollen knuckles as they headed for his 4x4. "You should ice that when you get home."

"We will," Roman blurted out. He bit his lip, wondering if he'd revealed too much.

Tristan's thoughtful gaze swung from Roman to Drake. "So, there *is* something going on between you."

Roman raised his chin defiantly, not caring about keeping his and Drake's relationship a secret anymore.

Tonight's events had made it clear what was important to him.

Roman startled when Drake suddenly stopped, turned, and hugged him tightly. "Drake?"

Drake shuddered. "I'm sorry I wasn't there for you," he whispered in Roman's hair. He pulled back and studied Roman with a tortured expression, a muscle jumping in his jawline. "That bastard almost—"

"Don't." Roman said shakily. "You *were* there for me, Drake. Just like you've been there for me these past few days." He rose on his tip toes and brushed his lips across Drake's, heedless of Tristan watching them. "You gave me the strength I needed to stand up to my father."

Roman still couldn't believe he'd challenged the

man who had terrorized him for over half of his life. When he'd stood on the steps of the RV and seen his father in front of him tonight, the fear that had gripped him had rapidly turned to burning anger.

Ash would have been so proud of me!

IN THAT MOMENT, ROMAN HAD SEEN HIS FATHER FOR who he truly was. A weak man who'd bullied others his entire life to make himself feel important. A coward who'd driven his wife away with his emotional and physical abuse and caused his own daughter to take her life. A flawed soul who relished in others' misery and stole their happiness from them.

Drake's eyes darkened with emotion. He took Roman's right hand and kissed his palm. "That was all you. You were amazing."

Warmth flooded Roman's face. "James had us take self-defense classes a few years ago. I just made sure to keep to an open space and use whatever I could around me as a weapon."

"Still, you were incredibly brave to stand up to him." Drake kissed Roman lightly.

"You guys realize we're still in a public parking lot, right?" Tristan drawled.

Roman flushed and glanced guiltily at the brightly-lit building behind them.

Drake sighed. "Remind me again why I called you?"

"'Cause I'm the only one of your friends not actively in a relationship right now and ergo, not having sex,"

Tristan muttered. "FYI, I have mixed feelings about that."

Despite Tristan's grumblings, Roman was grateful that he'd come to their aid. And he knew the other members of the Terrible Seven would have done the same, irrespective of what was going on in their private lives.

Roman and Drake got into Tristan's four-wheel drive and let him drive them to Drake's home. A pair of vehicles appeared in Tristan's headlights when he reached the end of Drake's driveway some fifteen minutes later.

Roman stared at James's Jaguar and Kurt's Porsche.

"What are they doing there?"

"I called James when I got to the station," Tristan said evasively.

Surprise jolted Roman. He frowned at Tristan's reflection in the rearview mirror. "How come you have James's number?"

Tristan shrugged, his expression deliberately vague. "I fixed his car when he came to Twilight Falls last week."

Drake gave Tristan a knowing look but didn't say anything.

"Great." Roman watched the men pouring out of the two vehicles with a sinking feeling. "The whole gang's here."

"A RE YOU SURE YOU'RE OKAY?" JAMES ASKED FOR THE tenth time as he paced Drake's kitchen.

Roman sighed. "Yes, I am. Now, sit your ass down. You're making me dizzy." He made a fresh ice compress and applied it to Drake's hand where they sat at the breakfast bar.

Drake did his best to ignore the laser-like stares the rest of Crazyknot were directing at them.

Kurt Taylor, Lewis Brandt, Hugo Strong, and Robbie Cantrell looked larger than life where they lounged around his kitchen.

It's a good thing I'm immune to famous people. Drake swallowed a dry smile. *Sam and Imogen would definitely faint if they were here right now though.*

"So, you're the guy doing Romi, huh?" Lewis muttered, chewing a pierced lip thoughtfully.

Roman cut his eyes to the drummer.

Drake arched an eyebrow. "Romi?"

"It's our nickname for Roman," Hugo volunteered.

Kurt frowned at Lewis. "What did we discuss about you saying the first thing that comes to your mind?"

Lewis rolled his eyes. "You told me to think before I speak, Granddad."

Robbie grinned. Hugo sighed.

James hesitated before coming over and squeezing Roman's shoulder lightly. "I'm sorry. I didn't realize I was being followed when I came to see you this week." Guilt darkened the manager's green eyes.

Roman's father had stalked James when he'd driven to Twilight Falls a couple of days back to warn Roman about his release from prison. He'd scouted out the estate and decided to make his move that night, slipping through the security gate after Gary and the rest of Drake's men had left for the day. With it being the weekend, Dusty Leyman had banked that no one would be coming to the estate over the following two days.

Drake knew Gary would kick himself when he found out what had happened. He didn't blame the foreman and neither did Roman.

Roman's father had had every intention of breaching the terms of his probation and seeking his son, wherever he might have been.

A shiver danced down Drake's spine when he thought about what could have happened if he hadn't turned up at the estate when he did. Leyman's actions had been those of a mad man and Drake feared he would have done more than just hurt Roman. The cops had found his tent in the woods nearby, along with ropes and tape.

Roman touched Drake's knee, as if sensing his inner turmoil.

Drake put his good hand on Roman's and gently squeezed his fingers.

"He's definitely doing Romi," Robbie said with an empathetic nod.

Roman scowled as the rest of Crazyknot murmured in agreement.

It was late by the time they retired for the night. Drake made up the guest rooms and the couches in the living room for his impromptu visitors and told them to help themselves to the kitchen and the toiletries in the bathrooms.

Roman's shoulders sagged when Drake closed his bedroom door behind them. He twisted on his heels and dropped his head on Drake's chest.

"God, they're exhausting."

Drake smiled and hugged him close. "They're just worried about you."

"I know." Roman looked up and worked his lower lip with his teeth. "It's just...well, not that I don't appreciate their concern, but we can't make out with them in the house."

Drake's cock stirred at the longing in Roman's voice. He glanced at the clean sheets on the bed and recalled his plans for them tonight.

"Why can't we make out?" Drake lowered his head and nipped teasingly at the tip of Roman's left ear.

Roman shivered and flushed. "You know very well why! I'm always loud when you make love to me."

"I'm sure we can do something about that," Drake drawled.

CHAPTER TWENTY-FIVE

Roman swallowed at Drake's wicked smile.

I can't believe he wants to have sex with James and the others in the house!

Despite Roman's misgivings, he couldn't deny the thrill that danced through him at the thought. His counter arguments flew out of his mind when Drake tipped his chin up with a knuckle and kissed him.

Roman sighed and melted into Drake, his hands rising to clasp the back of Drake's head. Drake slipped his tongue inside Roman's mouth and frenched him thoroughly as he walked him backward to the bed.

Air whooshed out of Roman when Drake pushed him down on the mattress. He landed with a bounce and bit his lip as Drake crawled onto the bed and crouched over him.

"Here's what I'm gonna do," Drake said in a silken voice, his blue gaze scorching Roman's body as he looked him up and down. "First, I'm going to strip us of our clothes. Then, I'm going to touch you and kiss you all over. After that, I'll blow your cock and rim your hole until you explode. Then, I'll fuck you. Nice."

Roman gasped when Drake traced a knuckle over his bulging erection.

"Slow." Drake leaned down, found Roman's nipple ring through his T-shirt, and gave it a playful tug, drawing a hiss from Roman's lips.

"And deep." Drake curled a hand under Roman's butt and squeezed his ass.

Roman's breathing accelerated as Drake's filthy words painted vivid promises across his mind.

Drake arched an eyebrow. "And Roman?" He gave Roman's ass another squeeze.

Roman swallowed. "Yeah?"

"You're forbidden from making a single, loud sound while I do all of that to you."

Roman's hole twitched. *Oh God!*

A sinful grin stretched Drake's lips when he registered Roman's reaction.

"In fact, I know the very thing that'll help keep you quiet."

Confusion washed through Roman when Drake got off the bed and went to his closet. He got a box down from a top shelf and removed a couple of items from inside it.

Roman's mouth went dry with lust and anticipation when he saw the red leather handcuff and ball gag Drake was holding.

"Why do you have those?" he mumbled.

"They're just a little something a former lover gave me."

Jealousy stabbed through Roman. "Did you use those on him?"

Drake smiled and shook his head. "He had his own." He came over to the bed, his expression turning serious. "Look, you've been through a lot tonight, so I understand if you don't want to do this."

Roman's breath shuddered out of him. "Drake?"

"Yeah?"

"I'm so fucking turned on right now, I swear I will hurt you if you don't do everything you just said you'd do to me," Roman growled.

Drake blinked before bursting out laughing. He laughed even more when Roman hushed him. He was still chuckling when he dropped the sex toys on the bed and divested Roman of his clothes. Drake removed a bottle of lube and a box of condoms from the nightstand, and stilled when Roman took hold of his hand.

"No condoms," Roman breathed.

Drake's eyes darkened. By the time he stripped and joined Roman, his cheeks were flushed with desire.

"Give me your hands."

Roman obeyed willingly. Cool leather kissed his heated skin as Drake cuffed his wrists. Drake put the key on the nightstand, took the ball gag, and placed it gently between Roman's lips, his gaze scorching.

"Bite down."

Roman did as Drake instructed. The silicone ball with its air holes felt surprisingly pleasant, the size just big enough to muzzle him without hurting his jaw. His heart thudded wildly against his ribs as Drake carefully secured the sex toy to the back of his head, their erections touching tantalizingly where Drake leaned over him.

Drake pushed Roman until he was flat on his back, nudged a pillow under his butt, and knelt between Roman's thighs to admire his handiwork, his erection at full mast.

Roman shivered where he lay with his legs parted and his knees bent. The feeling of submission was something he'd never experienced before during sex and it was turning his buttons on in all the right ways.

"I wonder what your fans would think if they saw you right now."

Roman shuddered as Drake trailed his fingers down his throat and chest, fingers pausing to twist and tug his nipple ring. Roman gasped and jerked, body arching into Drake's touch.

A feral light lit Drake's eyes at his wanton reaction.

"Would they revere your body like I'm doing?"

He closed his hand on Roman's aching cock and stroked him just like he liked it. Roman keened, his hole twitching and precum pooling out of his rigid shaft, the act of being cuffed and gagged making every inch of him ten times more sensitive.

"Would they expose the most sinful part of you to their hungry gaze?"

Oh God!

Roman clutched the pillow under his head as Drake hooked his hands behind Roman's knees and pushed his legs up in the air, lifting his lower body off the bed and stretching him wide.

Drake's gaze burned as he stared at Roman open and bare before him.

"Would they kiss you, right here?"

Ah fuuuuuck!

Roman's hole tingled and throbbed when Drake bent down and teased his hungry pucker with a furrowed tongue. He bit down on the ball gag to muffle his shout of pleasure, his toes curling in mid-air, and a jet of precum shooting from his dick and splashing onto his trembling belly.

"Would they want to sink their cocks into you, just like I'm going to?" Drake growled. He lowered Roman's legs and shifted until the head of his erection danced across Roman's hole.

Roman panted and rolled his hips, begging for exactly that.

Drake hissed as the motion rubbed Roman's folds up and down the underside of his rigid shaft.

He let go of Roman and flicked his tongue across the sensitive head of Roman's oozing cock. "It's too soon for that, Roman."

Then Drake did exactly what he'd promised. He touched Roman all over, his scalding lips and tongue following the passage of his hands as he slowly drove Roman out of his mind.

CHAPTER TWENTY-SIX

ROMAN'S MUFFLED MOANS AND KEENS ECHOED SWEETLY in Drake's ears as he lavished Roman's body with kisses and caresses, his heart thundering against his ribs.

His dick was so hard he was surprised he hadn't exploded yet.

A submissive Roman was even more of a turn on than Drake could ever have imagined. The way Roman gripped the pillow behind his head and danced his body close to Drake's mouth told Drake he was just as aroused by the titillating sex play.

Roman's mocha eyes were caramel pools of lust when Drake lifted his left foot and sucked his big toe into his mouth. His pretty cock pulsed and oozed out more precum, making a sticky pool on his belly.

By the time Drake finally took Roman's erection inside his mouth, Roman was a whimpering mess. He came with Drake's first suck, his cock throbbing and spurting, filling Drake's mouth and throat with his seed.

Drake swallowed it all hungrily, his tongue wrapping skillfully around Roman's throbbing organ. He licked and sucked Roman's quivering shaft until he'd milked the last drop of cum before letting go and turning his attention to Roman's ass.

Roman shuddered when Drake laid down between his spread thighs, sweat beading his face and chest as he looked dazedly along the length of his body at Drake.

Drake hooked Roman's legs over his shoulders, pressed Roman's thighs wide open, and started rimming him, his gaze locked on Roman's.

Roman's heels dug in Drake's back, a muffled scream leaving his throat. He rolled his hips and undulated on the bed as Drake prepared his hole for penetration, his motions pressing his entrance against Drake's mouth. Drake licked and sucked Roman's folds until they were soft and relaxed before pushing two lubed up fingers inside his body.

The way Roman's back passage tightened around him made Drake curse.

"Fuck!" Drake nipped the inside of Roman's right thigh with his teeth and earned himself a guttural moan. "I can't wait to sink my cock inside you!"

Drake finally slipped his fingers out of Roman and flipped him on his front. Roman trembled when Drake pressed his body down on him. Drake stretched Roman's arms above his head and clasped his hands. He rose slightly and nudged his cock between Roman's cleft, sweat dripping from his face and splashing onto Roman's back.

Roman moaned, spread his legs, and bent his knees, opening himself up to Drake. Drake cursed at the tantalizing view of Roman offering his body to him. He teased Roman's pucker with his dick before finally giving it to the lust raging through his veins. Drake's hand shook as he coated his aching cock with lube and guided the broad head to Roman's twitching entrance.

They both groaned when Drake parted Roman's folds and slipped inside an inch.

"Jesus!" Drake hissed. "I'll never get enough of this feeling! Your hole is the best thing my dick has ever tasted!"

Roman grunted and spasmed around him at the filthy words.

Drake grasped Roman's hands with one hand, braced the other next to Roman, and punched his hips forward in a slow, deep roll.

Roman whimpered as Drake stretched him deliciously open and filled him up to the hilt. Drake withdrew until the tip of his cock sat in Roman's entrance, cursing at the pretty way Roman's rim kissed his shaft. He thrust back in with a harsh grunt.

The way Roman convulsed and writhed beneath him told Drake he'd just come. Roman danced his hips against Drake's cock as he came, his shouts muffled by the ball gag and his hole clenching tightly around Drake's shaft.

Roman shivered and collapsed on the bed a moment later, aftershocks of pleasure shuddering through him. Drake kissed and nuzzled his nape, holding his body still by a sheer act of will.

All he wanted to do was to plunge his raging cock inside Roman and pound him into tomorrow.

Roman moaned as he came down from his high. He squeezed Drake's dick tentatively with his hole.

"Do you want more?" Drake murmured in Roman's right ear.

Roman nodded jerkily.

"Good." Drake slipped a hand under Roman and found his spent cock.

Roman whimpered as Drake started stroking his oversensitive flesh. Drake bit down on Roman's shoulder and started thrusting his hips again.

Roman hooked his feet on the back of Drake's knees, anchoring Drake to his body. His cock swelled and thickened between Drake's fingers as Drake stroked him, his cum making his shaft hot and slick.

Pleasure throbbed through Drake as he plundered Roman's hole with his stiff rod, feral grunts falling from his lips as he punched his hips savagely against Roman's ass.

The way Roman groaned and squeezed him with his hole told Drake he relished the savage mating just as much as Drake did.

Drake's belly clenched as his orgasm built into a hot, tight ball deep inside him. His movements grew more erratic and the bed rocked as his thrusts accelerated, the sounds of their wet flesh slapping together and their pants and groans heightening his arousal.

A guttural noise escaped Roman when he exploded in Drake's hand.

Drake bit his lip as Roman's hole spasmed violently around his cock, tipping him over the edge. He muffled his shout of pleasure as he climaxed, head dropping and hips pumping fitfully against Roman.

Roman's passage pulsed and throbbed around Drake as Drake filled him with his seed. Drake cursed when he saw his cum flow out of Roman's hungry hole. His erection was still raging when he pulled out of Roman and flipped him on his back.

Drake removed the ball gag from Roman's mouth, took his lips in a scorching kiss, and wrapped Roman's trembling legs around his hips.

"*Ah!*" Roman panted in Drake's mouth as Drake plunged back inside him with a single, powerful thrust. He hooked his cuffed wrists at the back of Drake's neck and hung on for dear life.

Drake withdrew and punched back in savagely.

"*Oh God!*" Roman keened, his back arching deliciously. "*Fuuuuck!*"

Drake swallowed Roman's cries as he did exactly that, fucking him hard and deep until they orgasmed again.

Cum oozed out of Roman in a thick trickle when Drake finally pulled his spent cock from his hole. He protested weakly as Drake climbed off the bed and lifted him in his arms.

"I can walk!" he gasped as Drake carried him into the bathroom.

"I know." Drake nuzzled his nose and kissed him. "I want to take care of you."

Roman flushed and buried his face in Drake's throat.

Drake's chest tightened, his heart swelling with an emotion he longed to deny.

CHAPTER TWENTY-SEVEN

Lewis grinned at Drake and Roman over brunch. "You guys fucked last night, didn't you? I can—*Ouch!*" He glared at Kurt. "What was that for?!"

Kurt lowered his hand where he'd slapped Lewis on the back of the head.

"I swear to God, I'll muzzle you one of these days."

Roman bit his lip hard. Drake took a leisurely sip of his coffee and squeezed Roman's thigh lightly under the table.

Their sex play with the ball gag and the handcuffs had continued in the bathroom and back in the bedroom for most of the night. Roman's hole throbbed pleasantly where he sat beside Drake. They'd taken a hot bath that morning and Drake had massaged his sore muscles while they soaked in the water. It was the only reason Roman could walk.

He really does know how to look after his lovers.

Roman's chest pinched slightly at that thought. Drake had had many sex partners in the past and would undoubtedly have many more after they ended their arrangement. He let that thought go and concentrated on eating.

Brunch became a noisy affair when Lewis and Robbie started a food fight over the last pancake. James and Kurt tried their best to keep them under control, to no avail.

"I am not cleaning this up," Drake declared in a haughty voice at the state of his kitchen.

"I'm sorry," Hugo said apologetically. "They always get like this when I make pancakes."

"Your pancakes aren't the problem." Kurt glared at an unrepentant looking Lewis and a petulant Robbie. "These assholes just need a good whipping."

Lewis's glazed over slightly. "Is it wrong that that kinda turns me on a little?" He grinned when grumbles and curses erupted around him.

Roman indicated Drake's cleaning closet. "The stuff you need is in there. Now, why don't you two children tidy up while the rest of us have coffee on the deck like the adults that we are?"

Lewis stuck his tongue out at them as they rose and headed outside.

The rest of the day passed in a blur. Roman and Drake showed the other four band members around the Strickland Estate while James had a conference call with Roman's lawyers regarding the previous night's incident. By the time they returned to Drake's house, James was wearing a grim expression of satisfaction.

"You father will be back in jail by Monday night,"

the manager told Roman. "And he won't be getting out any time soon."

Relief had Roman sagging against Drake.

Drake wrapped an arm around his shoulders, concern clouding his eyes. "You okay?"

Roman swallowed before nodding shakily. "Yes. I just—I hadn't realized how badly I wanted that to happen."

"So, what's there to do in this town on a Saturday night?" Lewis asked.

"FUCK. ME." IZZY STARED AT THE MEN STROLLING OVER to the table where she sat with Sam, Imogen, Wyatt, and Nathan. "It's Crazyknot and their hot, brooding manager."

James narrowed his eyes slightly. "I'm not sure if that's a compliment or an insult."

Izzy smiled impishly.

Imogen leaned sideways toward Sam. "Am I dreaming?" she mumbled in Sam's ear. "I'm dreaming, right?"

"Nope, it's really them," Sam muttered.

Drake ignored the shrewd glance she cast at him and Roman.

Lewis scratched his cheek, a teasing smile lighting his face as he studied Izzy. "Well, it would be rude to partake in sexual intercourse in public." He raked the brunette with his gaze, his smile widening. "Although, this place looks like it has a back room, so why don't we take a walk and—*Ouch!*"

Drake sighed as both Roman and Kurt stepped on Lewis's feet.

Wyatt frowned.

"Have I told you lately that the two of you are serious cock blockers?" Lewis grumbled.

"Izzy is off limits," Roman said. "And, FYI, the guy sitting next to her looking like he's about to stab you is her brother."

Izzy ignored Wyatt and grinned at Roman. "Oh, how sweet of you to defend me." She arched an eyebrow at Lewis. "I don't mind taking this little kid for a ride. Who knows, he might even learn some new tricks."

"*K-kid?!*" Lewis spluttered.

Kurt and the others grinned.

"Izzy," Wyatt groaned. Nathan chuckled.

"I'm gonna buy you a drink just for that," James told Izzy.

"You seen the other guys?" Drake asked Izzy as they pulled the next table and chairs over.

"Alex and Finn said they'd be late. They were gonna drop by the care home. The rest of them should be here soon." Movement near the door drew Izzy's attention. "Speak of the devil."

Drake twisted in his chair and saw Carter, Elijah, Hunter, Theo, and Tristan heading their way.

Imogen's eyes glazed over slightly. "I think my ovaries just exploded."

Sam patted her shoulder with a sympathetic expression.

An excited buzz filled *The Watering Hole* when the locals realized they had not one, but six stars in their midst. The flow of autograph seekers finally died down after an hour.

"Ten bucks says this is going to be all over tomorrow's local papers," Nathan drawled.

"It's already on social media," Sam murmured, scrolling through a feed on her phone.

"How come they aren't asking you for your autograph?" Hugo asked Carter curiously.

"You forget I grew up here," Carter said with a grimace. "Besides, half these people saw me run naked down Main Street when I was ten."

Elijah's eyes rounded. "You ran naked down Main Street?!"

Drake smiled in his beer as he recalled the incident. They'd stood outside Hunter's dad's hardware store and spurred Carter on.

Carter shrugged. "I lost a bet to Hunter."

"I still can't believe you couldn't get a kiss out of Daisy Dickson," Hunter said with a grin.

Carter narrowed his eyes. "Yeah, well, not everyone is sensitive to my charms."

"Daisy Dickson is gay," Sam said.

Shocked inhales erupted around the tables.

"No way," Hunter said. "But—she went out with half the guys on the baseball team in high school!"

Sam shrugged. "Well, she evidently decided dicks weren't her thing."

Carter turned an inquisitive eye on Hugo and the rest of Crazyknot. "What brings you guys here, anyway? This place is not your normal Saturday night scene."

Drake shared a guarded look with Tristan.

"We missed Roman, so we decided to visit," Kurt said lightly.

Tristan took a leisurely swig of his beer. "So, have you seen the place he's bought?"

Drake was grateful to Tristan for steering the conversation in a safe direction. Alex and Finn turned up a short while later and the rest of the evening ended on a pleasant note.

"You sure you want to go back to L.A. tonight?" Roman asked James and the others when they'd returned to Drake's house.

"Yeah, we've intruded enough on your space as it is," Kurt said.

"Besides, we just wanted to make sure you were okay." James turned to Drake. "Thank you. For letting us stay over and for what you did for Roman."

Drake shook the manager's hand and sensed that the man's hostility toward him had finally abated.

"We'll work on your songs until you come back," Hugo murmured as Roman hugged each of them on Drake's porch.

"And we'll call every day." Kurt closed his arms tightly around Roman. "Look after our Romi," he mumbled to Drake before letting go and climbing inside his car, his face suspiciously flushed.

Sadness clouded Roman's eyes as he watched his friends leave.

Drake took his hand. Roman leaned into him.

"I miss them already."

"You'll see them soon."

"Yeah." Roman sighed. "Another three weeks and I'll be back in L.A."

Drake ignored the heaviness that settled in his stomach at that news as they headed inside the house.

A FAINT BUZZING WOKE ROMAN. HE STIRRED AND opened his eyes where he lay in Drake's bed. Drake's arm tightened around his waist. He mumbled in his sleep and pulled Roman against his chest. Roman looked over his shoulder.

Desire danced through his veins as he studied Drake's sleeping face. He could feel Drake's dick nestled against his butt through his pajama bottoms.

Drake had insisted he get some rest last night and they'd gone to sleep without making love.

I'm sure we can rectify that situation this morning.

Roman was debating whether to slip under the sheets and rouse Drake with a blowjob when the buzzing came again. He lifted his head off the pillow and stared past Drake.

"Drake, your phone's ringing."

Drake blinked his eyes open. Awareness slowly returned to his face.

"Hey." He kissed Roman lightly before reaching

over to the nightstand. "Who the hell is calling so early on a Sunday?"

A second buzzing distracted Roman. His cell was ringing where he'd left it in his jeans, on the floor. He scooted across the bed and grabbed it from his pocket.

It was James. Roman frowned.

"Hi, Izzy," Drake mumbled as he answered his phone. "Do you even know what time it is?" He started rubbing a hand down his face and froze in the next instant, his eyes widening. "What?!" He looked over at Roman, the color draining from his skin.

A dark foreboding made Roman's heart thump. He took James's call, already knowing what it was that had made Izzy call Drake so early.

"How bad is it?" he asked James grimly.

"Bad." James's voice was full of tension at the other end of the line. "Someone leaked the Dusty Leyman story to the press. And there's a blurry snapshot of you and Drake kissing in the parking lot of the police station."

"Fuck!" Roman gritted his teeth. "It's gotta be one of the officers." He startled when Drake touched his shoulder. "Hold on, James." He put James on silent and swallowed as he met Drake's troubled gaze. "What's Izzy saying?"

"A reporter friend of hers from L.A. messaged her this morning to ask her if she knew about your attempted kidnapping yesterday." Drake frowned. "It's made the six a.m. entertainment news headlines."

"And the picture?" Roman asked, his stomach twisting.

A muscle jumped in Drake's jawline. "It won't take people here long to figure out it's me. It's the second reason why Izzy called. She could tell straightaway."

"Shit!" Roman climbed off the bed and started pacing the bedroom, his stomach a jumble of nerves. He got James back online. "James, Drake's with me. I'm gonna put you on speaker."

"Izzy, I'll call you later," Drake muttered before disconnecting his call.

"I'd love to say I didn't foresee this, but I can't," James said without preamble. "Drake, I'm sorry. The next couple of weeks are gonna be hell for you. Roman is used to the shit storm coming his way, although this is by far the worst scandal he's ever been involved in."

Roman's pulse jumped when Drake got out of bed and took him in his arms.

"Just tell me what I need to do, James." Drake pressed a kiss to Roman's forehead. "I'm not exactly a stranger to scandals. I saw what happened to Carter and Elijah when they first got together."

Roman shuddered and leaned into Drake.

Drake had every reason to be mad at him. This could damage his reputation and affect the business he'd worked so hard to build. The fact that he still intended to support Roman despite this had Roman's chest tightening with emotion.

"Okay, here's how we're gonna play this," James said.

"Is it true?" Gary asked Drake the second he stepped out of his Jeep on Monday morning. "Did that man attack Roman—" He stopped, his eyes rounding as Roman got out of the passenger seat. "Oh."

Lara strode past Gary and launched herself at Roman.

"Thank God you're okay!"

Roman startled and rocked back on his heels. He stiffened before closing his arms around the architect and returning her hug, his cheeks flushing.

"Did he hurt you?" Lara stepped back and scanned Roman's face anxiously.

"No." Roman shook his head. "Drake stopped him before he could."

Gary frowned at Drake's bruised knuckles. "Is that from where you hit the guy?"

"Yeah."

"Good," Gary said viciously.

Drake stared, a little shocked. It was his first time seeing Gary so angry. The man was normally as mild-mannered as a mole.

Regret clouded Gary's face as he turned to Roman. "The guys and I are really sorry. If it wasn't for us, he wouldn't have gotten inside the estate."

"Don't be," Roman said quietly. "My father would have found a way to get to me, regardless of where I was."

Lara sucked in air. A low murmur rose among Drake's men where they'd crowded behind Gary.

"So, that man really *is* your father?" Lara said hesitantly.

Roman grimaced. "Unfortunately, yes."

"And, er, you two are—?" Gary waved a vague hand at Drake and Roman.

"The word you're looking for is fucking, boss," someone said helpfully from the group behind him.

Gary scowled over his shoulder. "Jesus, Dan!"

"Roman could do so much better, right guys?" Dan said, unabashed.

The other men nodded.

"Totally."

"Drake is a grouch. A grouch with a big dick, but still, a grouch."

Lara snorted. Roman smiled.

Drake narrowed his eyes. "You guys are just begging for an ass-kicking, aren't you?"

Despite his grumbling, Drake couldn't help the relief that surged through him at his men's reactions. It had been the same when he'd brought Izzy and the Terrible Seven up to speed on the fresh scandal that had rocked Twilight Falls yesterday.

Drake wasn't so much worried about the town folks and his friends as he was about Roman. Twilight Falls had seen its fair share of gossip over the years and would barely bat an eyelid at the paparazzi who had descended on the place in the last twenty-four hours. He was more concerned about Roman's family history being dragged into the open.

As it was, the court order Roman had mentioned to Drake when he'd first told him about his past still stood. Bar someone interviewing Dusty Leyman directly or Roman deciding to divulge the information, the finer details of what happened to him as a teenager would remain locked behind masses of legal red tape. Of course, some of the information about Dusty Leyman was in the public domain and the records of his criminal activities were already all over the news.

The way James and Roman's agency had chosen to handle the scandal had proven to be a stroke of genius. Drake had been full of admiration when he'd seen the statement James had read out at a press conference yesterday afternoon.

The official story was that Roman came from a background of domestic violence and had been forced into an orphanage at age sixteen for his own protection from his criminal father. This provided the hungry press with the perfect backdrop to Roman's addiction problems and wild behavior in the early stages of his career.

Sales for Crazyknot's albums soared after the public realized what the rockstar had been through and big-name celebrities had flooded social media with messages of sympathy for Roman.

Drake's role in the event leading to Roman's father's arrest had proven another point of intense fascination. Roman had come out as gay years ago but had never been seriously romantically linked to anyone. That he'd kissed the man who'd come to his rescue was fodder the gossip channels couldn't get enough of. James hadn't formally named Drake during the statement and had asked the press to respect Roman's privacy during this difficult time.

This had only added fuel to the fire and

speculations were rife as to the exact relationship between Roman and the mystery man who'd saved him.

Drake frowned slightly as he watched Roman climb in the RV. He headed into the mansion with Lara and Gary for their scheduled meeting, his heart full of misgivings about what he had yet to reveal to Roman.

I should tell him about my past too, before the paparazzi find out about it and paste it all over the news.

CHAPTER TWENTY-NINE

THE NEXT TWO WEEKS PASSED IN A BLUR OF ACTIVITY AS Drake and his team worked diligently on the renovations. The scandal about Roman's father died down faster than any of them expected and Roman and Drake soon settled in a routine, having dinner and sleeping at each other's places most nights.

Sex with Drake remained as intoxicating as ever and Roman drowned in their love making every night. He discovered that Drake had a particular penchant for the black satin bedding in the RV and they spent countless hours making out on the silk sheets, so much so Roman bought a couple of sets for Drake's home. They went to visit Miles on several occasions and Roman got to know the rest of Drake's friends better over their poker games.

Roman often caught Drake watching him pensively when he thought he wasn't looking and couldn't help but feel that Drake wanted to tell him something but couldn't yet.

The final week of his planned stay in Twilight Falls came sooner than he'd expected. Roman invited Drake over for dinner on the Friday night and tidied the RV up as he waited for him to return to the estate.

Tension knotted Roman's stomach when he heard Drake pull up outside on his Harley. He intended to confess his feelings to Drake tonight and his nerves were making him slightly nauseous.

Drake knocked, opened the RV door, and climbed inside. "Hey."

Roman swallowed and smiled. "Hi."

They kissed before Drake put the bottle of non-alcoholic wine that Roman had come to favor in the refrigerator.

"So, what's on the menu tonight?" Drake looped his arms around Roman's waist and sniffed the air before arching an eyebrow at the pot simmering on the electric cooker. "Whatever it is, it smells incredible."

"I made paella." Warmth flooded Roman's chest at the easy way Drake held him. "It'll be ready soon."

Drake smiled. "You know, you're a far better cook than I'd thought you'd be."

Roman arched an eyebrow. "Is that prejudice I hear in your voice, Mr. Jackson?"

Drake chuckled. "Well, I *did* think you were a rich, spoiled brat when I first met you."

Roman dropped his hands to Drake's ass and pulled him closer. "Well, this *brat* sure has made you come a lot these past three weeks." He rose and nipped at Drake's throat with his teeth.

Drake groaned, his cock thickening and nudging

Roman's groin. "Don't. I really want to taste that paella."

Roman laughed and stepped out of his arms.

They took their time eating their meal and savored the wine Drake had brought. By the time they took care of the dishes and had coffee, it was past nine.

"So, what do you intend to do with me for the rest of the night?" Drake murmured, running his fingers lightly over Roman's knuckles where they sat opposite each other.

"Hmm, let me see," Roman said with fake seriousness. "We could catch a movie and have an early night for a change?" He bit his lip at the way Drake's face fell and burst out laughing. "I'm sorry! I couldn't resist."

"You tease." Drake rose and pulled Roman to his feet. He backed him against the table and tugged at his lower lip with his strong teeth. "I should punish you for that."

"Oh yeah?" Roman breathed, excitement sending blood surging through his veins. "What do you have in mind?"

Drake's eyes darkened. He glanced at the table.

The sinful smile that stretched his lips had Roman's cock twitching.

"I know just the thing." Drake stripped Roman of his T-shirt before unbuckling Roman's belt and working his jeans and boxers down and off his legs.

Roman shivered when Drake traced a finger along his growing erection.

"Pretty." Drake kissed Roman. "I can't wait to take you in my mouth."

Roman gasped as Drake curled his hand around his hardening length. Drake danced his lips down Roman's body and explored his skin and hot flesh while he stroked him.

Roman moaned and clutched the table when Drake played with his nipples, biting and stretching them with his teeth until they stung and throbbed.

"*Ah!*" he gasped, his head dropping back as Drake took the hard nubs inside his mouth and soothed them with his wicked tongue.

Drake slowly lowered himself to his knees, raining hot kisses all over Roman's abs and his trembling belly. His breath tickled Roman's trimmed pubes when he canted his mouth agonizingly close to Roman's straining erection.

"Drake," Roman mumbled.

"Yeah?"

"*Fuck!*" Roman cursed and curled his toes when Drake flicked his tongue lazily across the sensitive head of his cock. He grasped the back of Drake's head and guided his trembling organ to Drake's mouth. "Do it! Suck me. *Please.*"

Drake's eyes were blue pools of desire as Roman rubbed his dick across his lips. He held Roman's gaze and slowly opened them.

"*Oh!*" Roman's balls clenched and he almost came as he watched his cock disappear in the hot depths of Drake's mouth. "*Yes!* Like that!"

Drake let Roman's dick go with a wet pop before swallowing him again.

Roman groaned, his legs trembling at the teasing play.

Drake tortured him over the next few minutes, edging him close to his orgasm with his mouth and fingers before drawing back again and again, heedless of Roman's choked pleas.

"I want to come!" Roman finally whimpered, his body drenched in sweat and his cock tingling and throbbing. "Make me come, Drake!"

Drake growled, spun Roman around, and parted his cleft.

Roman cried out at the first hot flick of Drake's tongue against his pucker. He dropped a hand to his erection and started rubbing himself.

"No!" Drake growled, grabbing his wrist. "Hands on the table, Roman."

Roman bit his lip hard, his heart thundering against his ribs. He reluctantly obeyed Drake, knowing his climax would be even more spectacular if he did as Drake instructed.

Drake made a noise of approval.

Roman stiffened when Drake curled a hand around his right calf and lifted his leg.

"Put your foot on the chair," Drake commanded, nipping at Roman's butt cheek with his teeth.

Roman's dick throbbed as he did just that, the new position opening him wide for Drake's ministrations. Drake let out a hungry sound and closed his mouth on Roman's exposed pucker.

"Oh!" Roman keened. *"Oh God!"* His knuckles whitened where he gripped the table, pleasure arrowing through him where Drake sucked and licked him.

Drake stretched Roman's folds and poked his furrowed tongue inside, tasting him intimately.

"Fuck! *Yes!*" Roman cried out, his stiff cock oozing out precum.

Drake softened Roman's hole for long minutes before rising to his feet and grabbing the bottle of olive oil on the counter.

Roman flushed as he recalled their first sexual encounter in the RV. Except, this time, Drake's cock was going to be firmly lodged inside him instead of between his thighs.

Drake unbuckled his belt and drew his zipper down. His erection sprung free and slapped against Roman's butt.

"Take me, Drake," Roman begged, rolling his hips against Drake's cock. *"Now!"*

Drake cursed, coated his erection liberally with the oil, and thrust two slicked up fingers inside Roman. He stretched and loosened Roman for breathless moments before crowding Roman's back and entering him with a single, powerful thrust.

A guttural cry left Roman when the broad head of Drake's dick slipped through the tight band of muscles guarding his passage and pressed against his sweet spot, the burn and sting as pleasurable as it was painful.

Drake pulled back and punched his hips forward again with a feral sound, his hand clenching painfully on Roman's right thigh as he lifted his leg higher, opening him up for his penetration.

Roman came on Drake's third thrust, his cock exploding with pleasure so intense his vision flickered.

"Roman! Roman!" Drake mumbled as he thrust wildly in and out of him, his hot breath skittering across Roman's nape. He worked his hand around Roman's waist and caressed his still pulsing shaft.

Roman whimpered and dropped his head forward, inviting Drake's kiss. Drake pressed his mouth against Roman's flesh and licked and nuzzled him before biting down with savage possessiveness, as if he were claiming Roman as his mate.

Roman's dick soon hardened again as Drake fucked him hard and deep, the table rocking where they leaned against it. Drake's sweat dripped on Roman's naked back as he grunted and worked Roman's hole with his rod.

Roman gasped when Drake grabbed his left thigh and lifted his foot on the opposite chair. He leaned forward and grabbed the edges of the table with his hands as he found himself suspended in mid-air.

The new angle had Roman biting his lip in pleasure, Drake's pistoning cock reaching deeper inside him and coating his insides with precum.

"*Shit!*" Drake groaned. "So good!"

The way he stiffened and rose told Roman he was close to his orgasm.

Roman dropped his head forward and flushed when he looked down his body and witnessed Drake's penetration. He pressed his feet on the chairs and impaled himself repeatedly on Drake's cock, his breaths panting out of him and sweat dripping down his nose as he rose and fell.

Drake came on a loud shout, his fingers biting into Roman's flesh where he held his thighs.

Roman moaned, the feeling of Drake's throbbing dick shooting out cum deep inside him sending him over the edge. His body undulated in Drake's grip as he climaxed, his mouth open on soft keens and gasps.

They stilled against one another a moment later, Drake's thundering heart thumping violently against Roman's back. Drake carefully pulled out of Roman and lowered him to the floor.

Roman shivered as Drake's cum oozed down his inner thighs.

"Let's clean you up." Drake took Roman's mouth in a passionate kiss and tugged him to the bathroom.

They fell into bed after their shower and made love again before finally settling in each other's arms.

Roman's pulse quickened as he listened to the comforting beat of Drake's heart. He took a deep breath and was about to tell Drake what he'd been waiting to say to him all night when Drake spoke.

"There's something I've been meaning to tell you."

Roman stilled, hope stirring inside him.

"It's about my past," Drake murmured.

Roman's belly twisted. He looked up and met Drake's gaze in the half-light. "You don't have to, if you don't want—"

Drake kissed him, his lips lingering on Roman's mouth. "I want to. In fact, I'm surprised a reporter didn't get his hands on the story in the past couple of weeks." He smiled laconically. "It seems the people of Twilight Falls are determined to keep their dirty secrets close to their hearts."

Roman laid his head on Drake's chest and waited.

"My dad was the town drunk and my mom Twilight Falls' unofficial prostitute."

Roman drew a sharp breath. He met Drake's gaze and nearly cried at the age-old pain darkening the blue depths above him.

"No one spoke about it," Drake continued. "Not the adults, anyway. The kids weren't as forgiving. I was six the first time I heard the word whore. When I turned ten, I finally understood the meaning behind my mom's outings and why she and my dad never shared a bed."

Emotion clogged Roman's throat. In that moment, he wanted nothing more than to hold the little boy Drake was describing in his arms and tell him that everything was going to be okay.

"If it weren't for Alex and the others, I would have fallen into a dark place. They fought many of my battles alongside me." A sad smile tugged at Drake's mouth. "I lost count of the number of times Elaine had to patch us up after we had a fist fight with the older boys who used to say nasty things to me. It's part of the reason why our group gained its reputation."

"Where are your mom and dad now?"

"They got divorced shortly after my sixteenth birthday. Mom packed her things and went back to the East Coast. My dad stayed in Twilight Falls until I officially became an adult." Drake paused, his voice dull. "I haven't seen or spoken to them since I turned eighteen."

"I'm sorry." Roman squeezed his arms around Drake.

Drake hugged him back and pulled him up for a gentle kiss.

"I owed you the truth. And I wanted you to know why I've always avoided a serious relationship."

Roman stiffened. He dipped his head and pressed his face against Drake's chest, not wanting to hear the words Drake would say next.

"I don't think I can love someone. I thought I did with Alex for a while but, in hindsight, it was probably just passion." Drake hesitated. "This thing between us? It's much stronger than that. I know you're leaving on Monday, but I want to carry on seeing you when you come back to Twilight Falls."

Roman's heart shattered in a million pieces where he lay against the man he loved, knowing the confession that was lodged in his throat would stay there forever.

"Okay," he mumbled.

CHAPTER THIRTY

Drake hefted the banner higher. "Here?"

Tristan nodded. "Yeah, that looks good."

He helped Drake fix the strip to the arch separating Elaine's kitchen from her dining room. They stepped down from the chairs and looked around the gaily decorated house.

Miles was coming home today.

The whole of the Terrible Seven had been getting ready for his surprise welcome party all week. The pièce de résistance was the four-tier cake Elijah had baked, along with the other delicious food he'd prepared with Sam and Izzy the night before.

"He's gonna faint when he sees this," Nathan drawled where he was hanging streamers on the walls.

Hunter finished blowing up a balloon. "Yeah, well, we didn't get to do a party for his birthday the last twelve years, so he's having everything in one go." He indicated the enormous pile of gifts sitting at the end of Elaine's dining room with a proud grin.

Drake smiled. They'd bought Miles everything they would have gotten him for each of his birthdays and more.

Alex walked into the kitchen. "His room's ready."

Finn came in behind him, paint streaks on his hands.

Elijah brightened. "The mural's done?"

Finn smiled. "Yup."

Alex kissed Finn. "My husband's a genius."

Elijah sighed and covered Maisie's eyes. Maisie yanked his hands off her face and eagerly watched Alex and Finn lock lips.

"I'm gonna marry Uncle Miles when I grow up!" she told Elijah with a firm nod. She pointed at Alex and Finn. "And we'll do kissies, just like that!"

Carter almost dropped a glass.

"What? I thought you were gonna marry us when you grow up!!" He indicated himself and Elijah with a pained expression.

"Don't be silly, daddy," Maisie said sternly, causing several of them to bite their lips. "You're too old for me to marry."

"I hate to break it to you, kid, but your Uncle Miles is the same—" The rest of Hunter's words were muffled as Theo clamped a hand over his mouth.

The familiar sound of Elaine's Chevy rose from the driveway.

"Quick, hide!" Alex hissed.

They crowded behind the dining room door.

Footsteps sounded on the porch.

"Maybe we should install a ramp," Elaine said as she opened the front door.

"I'll be fine, Mom," Miles said. "Besides, I need the exercise."

"You're doing great," Izzy murmured reassuringly.

Drake and the others waited until the three of them came into the kitchen before jumping out from behind the door.

"*Surprise!*"

Miles rocked back on his heels at their welcome shouts, his eyes rounding and his hand tightening on the walking stick he held. He stared at the gaily decorated rooms before looking accusingly at Elaine and Izzy. "You knew?!"

"Of course." Izzy grinned. "It was my idea."

Miles flushed as everyone came to hug him.

Elijah brought out the cake he'd made and Elaine lined it with candles. Laughter erupted when Maisie helped Miles blow them out. The rest of the afternoon passed in a flurry of laughter and happy moments.

The sun was low in the sky when Drake and the others finally got ready to leave. Though he'd gotten some questions concerning Roman, no one had probed Drake too deeply about his relationship with the rockstar. Roman's return to L.A. and news of Crazyknot recording a brand new album had been all over the entertainment channels a fortnight ago, finally putting to rest the speculations about the mystery man who'd saved Roman from his criminal father. Even though Drake had spoken to Roman most days since he'd left Twilight Falls, Roman hadn't come back to town yet.

Miles caught up with Drake as he climbed onto his Harley.

"Hey, thanks again for today."

Drake smiled. "No problem. Everyone wanted to celebrate your homecoming."

Miles pulled a face. "I think I've had enough celebrations to last me a lifetime. It's been a non-stop party at the care home since I woke up."

Drake chuckled at that.

Miles's eyes darkened with a nameless emotion. "Drake?"

"Yeah?"

"I—" Miles stopped, his gaze skittering away. "It's nothing."

Drake frowned slightly. "Hey, you okay?"

"Yeah." A sad smile curved Miles's mouth. "I'm happy for you."

Drake startled when Miles suddenly hugged him. "Are you sure you're really okay?" he murmured, squeezing Miles back. "You're acting kinda strange."

Miles drew back, his cheeks flushed. "No, I'm not okay. But I will be. Eventually."

Concern gnawed at Drake. "Is it your health? Are you hurting somewhere?" He stiffened. "Is it your head?"

Miles blew out an exasperated sigh. "I swear, you're worse than Izzy. Don't worry, it's nothing physical. I just...need to wrap my mind around everything I've missed out on while I was asleep."

A wave of sorrow swept over Drake at the haunted look that dawned on Miles's face. "We missed you. So much." He squeezed Miles's hand. "We're here for you. Whatever you need, man."

Miles nodded shakily, tears glimmering in his eyes. Drake hugged him again before taking off, his chest tight with emotion.

A familiar Ducati appeared in the Harley's headlight when he rode down his driveway. His heart lurched.

Roman was sitting on his porch.

Drake parked his motorcycle and headed briskly over, elation quickening his pulse; he hadn't realized just how much he'd yearned to see Roman until he was there, in front of him.

"You should have gone inside. I gave you a key."

Roman rose and shook his head, a sad light in his eyes. "I can't do that."

A sudden premonition shot through Drake at Roman's expression. Trepidation coiled inside him, slowing his steps.

"Roman?" He stopped a couple of feet from the rockstar, too scared to draw any closer.

Roman took a shaky breath. "I love you, Drake."

A buzzing noise filled Drake's ears.

"I've been in love with you since the first week we got together." Roman's eyes glittered in the night. "I'll still be in love with you years from now." He swallowed heavily. "That's why we should break up."

The world tilted dizzyingly around Drake. "What?"

"I thought I could do what you'd suggested and carry on seeing you," Roman said quietly. "But I want more than just stolen moments with you. I don't want this to be a casual arrangement with a finite end point. I want *you*, Drake. Forever."

Drake froze, too stunned to speak.

Roman's shoulders sagged at his silence. He removed the spare key Drake had given him from his jacket, took Drake's hand, and placed it gently in Drake's palm.

"I know." Roman rose and brushed his lips across Drake's mouth, tears glimmering in his mocha eyes and his voice quivering. "I know you can't love me back. That's why I need to let you go. Before my heart breaks even more and I can't put the pieces back together."

Roman let go of Drake's hand and walked past him.

The sound of the Ducati faded behind Drake. How long he stood there staring at the spare key in his palm, he didn't know. It wasn't until a light rain started falling that Drake finally shivered and stirred.

He blinked at the darkness around him and swallowed hard.

Before he knew it, Drake was back on his Harley.

The rainfall had intensified by the time he pulled up outside Alex and Finn's place. Drake pounded on their front door until Alex opened it with a full-blown scowl. He vaguely registered Alex's messy clothes, aware he'd likely interrupted the couple while they were making out.

"What the—?" Alex's frown faded. "Drake? What's wrong?!"

"What do I do?" Drake said hoarsely.

"Alex?" Finn came up behind his husband. "What's the matter?"

Alex took Drake's arm and tugged him inside the foyer.

Drake blinked at the two men, his clothes dripping water all over their floor.

"Did something happen with Roman?" Alex asked stiffly.

"He left me." Drake wiped a hand down his face and startled when he tasted the saltiness of tears on his lips. "Roman left me." His voice broke on his last word.

Alex exchanged a worried glance with Finn before taking Drake in his arms and stroking his back with soothing motions.

CHAPTER THIRTY-ONE

THE NOISE OF THE CLAPPING CROWD AND THE LOUD music reverberating through the auditorium thumped steadily in the distance. Roman straightened his clothes and took a last look at himself in the mirror of Crazyknot's dressing room.

"You ready?" Kurt said.

Roman turned and gazed at his band. They were wearing matching white T-shirts and black jeans, with Roman's wine-red leather jacket the only item making him stand out as the lead singer.

He smiled and tucked his earpiece in place. "Let's do this."

They formed a circle, held hands, and yelled, *"Crazyknot rocks!"*

James opened the door just as they threw their hands up wildly in the air.

"That war cry never gets old," he drawled. "Now, how about you get your asses out there and show these people a good time?"

Roman led the way out of the dressing room, a familiar buzz building in his veins. He always got a little nervous before a performance, but he knew he'd be okay once he started to sing.

Today was the first day Crazyknot would be live on stage since the scandal about Roman's father broke out. They'd finished recording their latest album in record time and intended to play two songs at the charity gig James had chosen for them to perform at tonight, ahead of the album's release next month.

The concert was for victims of domestic abuse and Crazyknot was one of several big names appearing tonight. The organizers were hoping to raise at least a million dollars. Judging from the size of the crowd and their response, they would easily achieve that goal and more.

Being busy has been good for me.

It had been ten days since Roman had gone to Twilight Falls and told Drake he was breaking up with him. Though his heart was still raw from losing the man he loved, diving into the studio and spending time with his band had helped distract him from the scar in his soul.

They said time healed all wounds.

Roman only hoped this wound would eventually heal too, just like the scar he'd carried in his heart over his dead twin sister had started to mend ever since he fell in love with Drake.

Dazzling lights washed over him and his band when they walked out into the auditorium moments later. The energy of the crowd was a living thing that wrapped around Roman and his friends and brought smiles to their faces.

Roman strolled up to the microphone and removed it from the stand.

"Hello, people of L.A.!" He waved and strolled to the edge of the platform.

The crowd roared so loudly the stage trembled.

Roman grinned. "That's what I like to hear. We have two very special songs to share with you tonight." He paused, his heart clenching slightly. "As you're probably aware, the past month hasn't been easy for me. But, you know what they say." He arched an eyebrow. "Misery breeds inspiration."

Laughter broke out among the concert fans watching him avidly.

"We love you, Roman!" someone shouted.

A pair of red silk panties sailed out from the gloom and landed at Roman's feet. He leaned down and picked them up with a chuckle.

"Oh, wow. Someone out there must be feeling the breeze right now." Roman squinted at the crowd. "But you guys know I'm more into jockstraps than panties, right?"

Lewis put his drum sticks down, rose, and started unbuckling his jeans, much to the crowd's amusement.

"Down, Cujo," Kurt warned. He hooked his guitar over his neck and strummed out the first note of their new song.

And with that, Crazyknot's performance started and the crowd went wild.

❧

DRAKE STOOD AT THE BACK OF THE AUDITORIUM, HIS heart in his mouth.

The man on the stage was someone he'd never seen before.

Gone was the vulnerability he'd often seen in Roman's eyes and the air of fragility that always surrounded the rockstar.

This Roman was confident, loud, and oozed sex appeal out of his very pores.

Drake's cock twitched at the sultry tones leaving Roman's throat as he and his band worked their fans into a frenzy. Though he'd often witnessed Roman humming when he was working on his songs, this was the first time Drake was hearing him sing live.

Every filthy moan and cry Roman had ever made for Drake echoed in his ears and made desire coil in his veins.

"Come on," Alex shouted in Drake's ear. "Izzy's got the backstage pass. We need to go, now!"

Drake followed Alex out of the crowded auditorium.

Izzy was waiting for them in the hall outside. She waved a lanyard with a visitor card at the end of it, a wide grin splitting her face.

"You owe me big time for this."

Drake took the pass and kissed her. "I do," he told a shocked Izzy once he'd lifted his mouth off hers. "And if I wasn't gay, I'd marry you."

"Damn," Izzy mumbled, touching her lips.

"Bastard's a great kisser, isn't he?" Alex said with a sigh.

Izzy shoved a bouquet of red roses in Drake's hands.

Drake took a deep breath and adjusted his tie. "Wish me luck."

Alex smiled. "Go get him."

Drake headed down the hall to where a couple of security guards stood in front of the backstage access doors. They checked him over and let him through.

His mind buzzed with a dozen thoughts as he followed the directions Izzy had given him. The last ten days had been an eye-opening experience for him in more ways than one. He'd spent that first night at Alex and Finn's place and had woken up the next morning to find Izzy holding a council of war with the couple.

"You look awful," Izzy had told Drake when he'd walked into Alex and Finn's kitchen.

"Thanks," Drake had muttered as he'd poured himself a coffee.

"So, when are you going to get that miserable look off your face and admit that you've fallen for Roman?" Alex had asked with a raised eyebrow.

Drake had stilled then. "You of all people know why I can never fall in love," he'd said with a frown.

"Wow," Izzy had said leadenly. "You were right," she'd told Alex. "He's a bona fide idiot."

"He really is," Finn had murmured.

"Love isn't something you can control, Drake," Alex

had said in a hard voice. "And it sure as hell doesn't obey your will. You've got two choices. Either you stick to your ridiculous notion that you can never make someone happy and stay miserable and alone for the rest of your life, or you stop acting like a coward and take a chance on what your heart is screaming at you to do."

Drake smiled faintly as he went in search of Crazyknot's dressing room.

Who would have thought Alex would be giving me love lessons one day?

Although he'd wanted to come to L.A. to see Roman sooner, it was Izzy and Alex who'd advised him that tonight's gig would the perfect time and place to surprise Roman.

James was standing outside the band's dressing room when Drake finally found the place. He looked up from checking his phone and sucked in air.

"What the heck are you doing here?" James's gaze dropped to Drake's clothes and the bouquet. He gaped. "Wait. Is this what I think it is?!"

§

ROMAN GAVE A FINAL WAVE TO THE CROWD AND CAUGHT the bottle of water a crew member lobed at him as he and Crazyknot headed backstage. He dabbed his face with a towel and frowned slightly.

"I think we should rework the last lines of the second song."

Kurt slapped him on the back. "Will you just enjoy

the moment? We just brought the house down and you're worrying about a string of words."

Roman pouted. "They're important words."

Kurt looped an arm around Roman's shoulders and rolled his eyes. "Yeah, yeah."

They chatted and joked as they walked farther backstage.

James was standing outside their dressing room when they approached it, a strange expression on his face.

"Hey, guys. Can we give Roman a moment? There's someone in there waiting to speak to him."

Roman slowed to a stop, puzzled. "Who's waiting for me?"

"It's a kid the charity chose to meet with you," James said with a shrug.

Roman frowned and glanced at his equally bewildered band members.

"Then, shouldn't we all meet him?"

James sighed. "No. He wanted to meet you alone."

Suspicion coiled through Roman. "There had better not be an inflatable sex doll in there, like that time we toured in France."

Lewis snorted.

"Just, get in there!" James grabbed Roman, opened the dressing room, and pushed him inside before slamming it shut in his face.

"I bet it's an inflatable sex doll," Roman muttered under his breath as he twisted on his heels.

He rocked to a stop, his whole world turning upside down when he saw the man in the dark grey morning suit and wine-red silk tie sitting on the stool opposite him.

"Hi, Roman," Drake said quietly.

"What—" Roman stopped and swallowed, "what are you doing here?! How did you even get backstage?!"

"Izzy got me a pass." Drake rose to his feet and came over.

Roman backed away, his heart clenching painfully. "No. Stop." His face crunched up. "Goddamnit, I was finally starting to breathe without you! Why are you doing this—"

He gasped when Drake cradled his face and took his mouth in a sweet kiss. Roman clenched his fists on Drake's shoulders, fully intending to push him away. But he couldn't. Not when Drake was touching him as if he were the most precious thing in the world.

It wasn't until Drake lifted his mouth off his and gently wiped away the tears on his cheeks that Roman realized he was crying.

Drake stared into Roman's eyes, his own blazing with fierce emotion. "I love you, Roman."

CHAPTER THIRTY-TWO

ROMAN FROZE, HIS PUPILS DILATING BENEATH DRAKE. The shock and hurt reflected in his caramel gaze made Drake curse himself all over again.

"I'm sorry." Drake dropped his forehead against Roman's and kissed the tears on his eyelashes. "For being a fool. For hurting you."

Roman trembled, his hands twisting on the material of Drake's jacket.

"I love you. I've probably loved you since the first time I saw you, at Carter and Elijah's wedding." Drake paused and closed his eyes. "I was just too much of a coward to accept my feelings for you."

Roman's fingers danced lightly on Drake's face. Drake opened his eyes.

The tremulous smile lighting up Roman's face punched him in the gut and choked his breath.

"God, you are *so* beautiful." Drake caressed Roman's lips with a reverent touch and promised himself he would do everything in his power to make this man happy if he accepted him. "I love you so damn much!"

Roman moaned and clutched Drake's shoulders, rising to seek his mouth. Their lips clashed in a torrid kiss, their hands touching and stroking each other's bodies as if they couldn't believe they were both there right now.

It was some time before they let each other go, their chests heaving with their heated breaths.

"What made you change your mind?" Roman mumbled.

"Seeing you walk away." Drake smiled laconically. "When I realized I'd lost you, every damn, stupid reason I'd ever given myself for not accepting my feelings for you just seemed like so much bullshit."

Roman chuckled.

"The night you broke up with me, I went to Alex and Finn's place."

Roman inhaled sharply. "Alex?"

Drake smiled at the jealous light that flashed in his gaze. "It wasn't like that. I was crying and I needed to talk to someone who knew me better than I knew myself. Someone who could tell me what I should do to avoid making the same mistake I'd made in the past."

Roman paled. "You cried?"

Drake grimaced. "Yeah. Big, fat man tears."

Roman chewed his lower lip, guilt darkening his eyes. "I'm sorry."

Drake sighed and took him in his arms. "That's one of the many, *many* things I love about you. The fact that you're saying sorry to the man who was a complete asshole to you."

"You were an asshole, weren't you?" Roman mumbled in Drake's chest.

"Totally."

Roman raised his head. "Hmm, Drake. I've been meaning to ask you." He glanced curiously at the dressing table. "What's with the morning suit and the roses?"

"Oh." Drake extricated himself from Roman's arms and went over to grab the bouquet, his pulse accelerating with a bout of nervousness.

Roman gasped when Drake turned and removed a pretty velvet box out of his jacket. "What are you—?"

Drake cleared his throat and got down on one knee, palms sweaty and heart thundering as he opened it, revealing the beautiful, platinum band inside.

There was every chance Roman would reject his proposal. They'd never discussed their personal views on marriage and, truth be told, Drake had not believed in the institution for a long time. But he only had to look at his closest friends and their relationships to realize that just because his parents' marriage had been a disaster didn't mean his would be too.

"Drake," Roman whispered, his face flushed.

The hope burning in Roman's eyes was all the encouragement Drake needed to make the final commitment to the man standing before him.

"Roman Campbell, will you grant me the honor of becoming—?"

The door opened abruptly under the weight of the

five figures who'd been leaning against it. They tumbled inside the dressing room and crashed unceremoniously onto the floor.

Lewis groaned at the bottom of the pile of bodies.

"I told you assholes not to push," James grumbled where he lay on top.

The four band members and their manager got up under Drake and Roman's narrow-eyed stares.

"So, did he say yes?" Kurt asked Drake eagerly as he scrambled to his hands and knees.

"I didn't get a chance to finish proposing," Drake said darkly.

Roman scowled.

The five men rose to their feet, their expressions somewhat abashed.

"Well, don't let us stop you," James said, dusting himself off.

Drake and Roman gazed at them as if they'd lost their minds.

"Look, we're the closest thing you've got to a family and we should be here for this," Kurt argued.

Roman's shoulders sagged. He met Drake's gaze. "They're right."

Drake sighed and smiled. "Okay." He cleared his throat again. "Dear Roman Campbell—and irritating family—"

"Hey!" Kurt protested.

Drake ignored the guitarist, his gaze locked on the man in front of him.

"Will you grant me the honor of becoming my husband?"

Roman's chin quivered. "Yes," he breathed.

Every eye in the room misted over when Drake took Roman's left hand and slipped the ring on his finger.

"Oh shucks, you guys!" Lewis wailed. "You're gonna make me bawl!"

Kurt passed him a tissue.

CHAPTER THIRTY-THREE

Drake and Roman tumbled through the front door of Roman's condo, lips locked and hands frantically touching one another.

"This place is kinda cool," Drake mumbled distractedly. "You should show me around."

"This is the kitchen," Roman panted as Drake walked him backward through the open plan living area, his hands busy on Drake's belt buckle. "And that's the dining room." He pulled Drake's zipper down and freed his erection.

Drake groaned as Roman caressed his stiff length. "Keep going." He shrugged Roman's jacket off his shoulders.

"There's the living room. And—*ah!*" Roman bit his lip as Drake found his nipple ring through his T-shirt and gave it a playful yank. "There's a pool and a hot tub out on the deck. *Oh!*" This time, Drake had found Roman's erection through the material of his jeans and was rubbing it roughly with the heel of his palm.

"Hmm," Drake murmured as he rapidly divested Roman of his boots and clothes before stripping out of his own, leaving a mess on the floor. "We should explore that hot tub later. Now, where's the bedroom?"

"It's down that hall." Roman gasped when Drake grabbed the back of his thighs and lifted him up against him. He locked his legs around Drake's hips and looped his arms around Drake's neck, a sultry sigh falling from his lips as their erections kissed.

Drake took Roman's mouth with his own and headed for the bedroom. He paused when he entered it and arched an eyebrow.

"Red satin sheets?"

Roman flushed. "I wanted to forget about the black ones."

Drake sobered and pressed a passionate kiss to Roman's lips. "I'm sorry." He smiled faintly. "I bet you look even sexier on red satin sheets."

Roman flushed as Drake carried him over to the bed and laid him down. His pulse raced erratically when Drake stood back and studied him with a scorching stare.

Drake dropped a hand to his straining cock and gave himself a brisk rub.

"I was right," he growled as he knelt on the edge of the mattress. "You look fucking unreal right now."

Roman shivered, his dick twitching and his hole contracting in anticipation. Drake crowded him on the bed, took his mouth in a scalding kiss, and pressed down on him.

They groaned as their bodies touched intimately.

"I've missed you." Drake danced his lips lovingly all over Roman's face and down his throat. "I've missed you so damn much!"

Roman's chest tightened at the adoration in Drake's voice and in his eyes. He still wanted to pinch himself to make sure he wasn't dreaming. That this was really happening.

The weight of the unfamiliar ring on his finger was all he needed to know that his wildest wish had come true. That Drake was here, with him. And that they never intended to let each other go.

Desire raged through Roman as Drake worshipped his body with his fingers and his mouth, his touch as possessive as it was tender. Drake kissed and caressed Roman's chest and belly before settling between his thighs and swallowing his trembling cock in a single, hungry gulp.

"Oh! *Oh God!*" Roman gripped the pillow under his head and arched his back as Drake sucked him with powerful motions of his jaw. "*Yes!*"

It wasn't long before Roman climaxed, his heels digging into the bed as he undulated and spilled his cum inside Drake's mouth and throat, his cries of ecstasy echoing around the bedroom. Sweat beaded his face and body when he collapsed down, his body quivering and twitching with sharp aftershocks of pleasure.

Drake put two fingers inside his mouth and slicked them with Roman's cum before spreading Roman's trembling thighs and finding his pucker.

Roman held Drake's burning gaze as Drake stroked

and circled his folds, teasing his opening. He tilted his hips, silently begging Drake for more.

Drake gnashed his teeth and pushed inside his body.

"*Hmmm*," Roman hummed, closing his eyes briefly as Drake stretched him deliciously open. He rolled his hips against Drake's hand. "More!"

Drake cursed at Roman's sultry demand and started plundering Roman's back passage with deep thrusts, his fingertips finding the soft bump of his prostate over and over again. He closed his other hand on Roman's cock and soon brought him to another erection.

Roman reached down and touched Drake's rigid shaft, his heart thumping wildly in his chest and lust a tight ball clenching his belly.

"I want this inside me!" Roman met Drake's heated gaze and gave Drake's rod a brisk rub. "Please! Fuck me, Drake!"

"Shit!" Drake let Roman go and found the bottle of lube in Roman's nightstand. He gritted his teeth as he slicked up his cock, moved across the bed, and settled with his back against the headboard. "Come here."

Roman straddled Drake, his dick oozing precum and his mouth dry with excitement. Drake pushed two lubed fingers inside Roman and scissored and stretched him before grabbing his hips and guiding him to kneel over his erection.

Roman panted as Drake slowly lowered him down onto his cock. He grabbed his ass and stretched his opening when the broad head kissed his folds.

"*Aaaah!*"

Roman's cry was echoed by Drake's lustful groan as he entered Roman's back passage. Roman rolled his hips in gentle rocking motions as he swallowed Drake's erection, his insides burning and stinging with pleasure pain.

They both gasped when Roman was fully seated on Drake's groin.

Drake leaned in and kissed Roman.

"Grab the headboard and fuck yourself on my cock," he breathed against Roman's lips, his gunmetal eyes blazing with desire.

"Shit," Roman moaned, his dick twitching hungrily at the filthy command. He grasped the headboard on either side of Drake's shoulders and moved his legs until he squatted on Drake's erection with his feet pressed down on the bed.

"Fuck!" Drake grunted as Roman rose off his rod and slowly impaled himself again.

Roman's body tensed with growing pleasure as he did exactly as Drake had ordered and rode Drake, the wicked, wet sounds their mating flesh made as Drake's dick moved in and out of his hole so intoxicating he was surprised he didn't explode right away.

Drake found Roman's nipples with his teeth and worked them with sensuous tugs and bites, his fingers biting into Roman's butt cheeks where he held him. He worked a hand around to Roman's bobbing cock and started rubbing him, his thumb dancing across the sensitive head in teasing circles.

The triple stimulation soon had Roman climaxing with sweet violence.

Drake swallowed Roman's hoarse shout and starting thrusting up as he chased his own orgasm.

Roman whimpered and sobbed as Drake stroked his sensitive cock. His dick trembled and thickened once more, the feeling of Drake's rod massaging his sweet spot providing all the stimulation he needed to achieve another erection.

This time, Drake waited until they were both ready before he sent them over the edge.

Roman's heart trembled with love as Drake gripped his hips and came on a loud shout, his face flushed and his mouth open on his sound of ecstasy. Roman convulsed above Drake, low moans falling from his lips as he spurted cum all over Drake's chest and belly. Drake sank his teeth in Roman's shoulder and pumped his hips, his motions rocking the bed as he filled Roman's hole with his thick seed.

Blood buzzed in Roman's ears when they collapsed against one another a moment later, their hearts thundering where their chests kissed.

"I'm sorry, but I don't think you're going to be able to walk tomorrow," Drake panted against Roman's throat. "I hope you haven't got anything important lined up."

Roman's hole contracted at the filthy promise and drew a groan from both of them.

"I don't," he chuckled breathlessly. "Oh, man. You've got it bad, huh?"

"So bad." Drake looked up and nuzzled Roman's nose lovingly. "Now, how about you show me the bathroom so I can clean you up before we test that hot tub?"

Roman laughed, his passage squeezing Drake and drawing another heartfelt groan from him.

THE END

Can a brooding, tattoed mechanic save a vulnerable rock band manager?
Get Tristan (Twilight Falls 6)

Have you read the Nights series yet? Find out if Gabe Anderson accepts Cam Sorvino's promise of one night of mindless pleasure to help him overcome his phobia of intimacy!
Get One Night (Nights 1)
Turn the page to read an extract now!

ONE NIGHT (NIGHTS #1)
SPECIAL PREVIEW

CHAPTER ONE

WHAT THE HELL AM I DOING HERE?

Gabe Anderson scanned the crowded club in the mirror opposite the bar before looking down into his scotch with a self-deprecating smile. This had seemed like such a great idea an hour ago, when he'd been staring at an empty weekend in an even emptier apartment.

Saron was located in a side alley, a short walk from Shinjuku's main club strip. Despite its somewhat shady location, the place oozed style.

Gabe had hesitated when he'd seen the suited doorman guarding the entrance and wondered if access was by invitation only. He only knew of *Saron* from overhearing his clients mention it a few nights ago. From what he'd made of their excited conversation, it was *the* place to hang out in Shinjuku if you were of a particular sexual inclination.

The doorman had checked Gabe over for all of three seconds before wordlessly unclipping the rope from the stanchions framing the steel doors. He had obviously passed some kind of test, though what it was he didn't know.

Beyond a foyer with a cloakroom manned by a male attendant who looked like he'd walked straight out of a *GQ* shoot were a set of shallow steps leading to a wide, sunken floor.

Despite the butterflies churning his stomach, Gabe had stopped and stared appreciatively at the decor. As a consultant for one of Chicago's biggest design firms, he could tell how much money had gone into giving *Saron* its unique look. The club was drowned in deep reds, dark purples, and rich earth tones. Scattered across the oak floor were Brazilian cherry wood tables and armchairs boasting plush velvet upholstery and satin cushions. Discrete booths dotted the walls and afforded privacy to those who needed it, although the muted lighting provided enough of that as it was. A polished mahogany counter with wine-red leather and walnut stools ran the length of the bar on the right.

At the far end of the room, a woman in a black cocktail dress stood on a raised podium. She was crooning a song in a sultry, deep voice, her eyes closed and her glossy ruby lips glistening in the mellow spotlight. Behind her, cymbals vibrated gently, a piano tinkled, and a saxophone hummed, the sounds somehow rising above the voices of the men packing the place.

It was as he'd made his way to the bar that Gabe had realized why the doorman had let him in. From the looks of the club's patrons, *Saron* catered exclusively to an upscale clientele. He was willing to bet a week's wages none of the suits in the place cost less than five hundred dollars.

"Ah, fresh meat."

Gabe froze in the act of sitting on a barstool, his gaze swinging up to meet a pair of amused green eyes on the other side of the mahogany counter.

"Excuse me?" he said stiffly.

The bartender, a striking blond in a slate, silk tuxedo vest and crisp white shirt, flashed him a grin.

"I've not seen you around these parts before. What will it be?"

Gabe swallowed, wondering whether the man had seen straight through him and grasped the reason he had come to *Saron*.

"What will what be?" he mumbled, unable to mask the apprehension in his voice.

The bartender pursed his lips and observed him with a shrewd expression before leaning across the counter.

"Relax," he murmured in Gabe's left ear. "I can tell it's your first time in a place like this. If you keep up that deer-in-the-headlights look you've got painted across that pretty face of yours, you're gonna be a target for every sleaze ball in this club. And, trust me, they might be wearing thousand-dollar ensembles, but some of these assholes are nothing but dirty pigs in suits."

An involuntary bark of laughter left Gabe's lips at the mental image the bartender's words had conjured. The sound carried along the counter, drawing stares.

The knot of tension that had been sitting between Gabe's shoulder blades ever since he ventured into Shinjuku eased as he smiled at the bartender.

"I've never been called pretty before."

The guy winked.

"Trust me, you're the hottest thing on legs in this place right now. Besides me, of course."

Gabe chuckled and ordered a scotch, his confidence boosted by the compliment.

Two months had passed since he'd relocated to Tokyo from Chicago. When his bosses had sprung the offer on Gabe in early spring, the chance of a fresh start in a place void of the dark memories that had plagued him for eight years was too much of an attractive proposition for him to reject. He'd left Chicago with two suitcases and five crates full of books and artwork, the only things he had to show after a decade in the city.

Though he had been prepared for the culture shock, life in Tokyo had still come as a surprise, albeit an invigorating one. He had always had an interest in the country and its intoxicating mix of traditional and contemporary customs ever since he made his first business trip to the Japanese branch of the firm four years ago.

Luckily, his new position suited him to a T. He had thrown himself into his first assignment with his usual drive and passion, leading the team under him to make good on a project, one which his predecessor had only made a half-assed attempt to complete. He had delivered on time, on budget, and on schedule, despite the nearly impossible deadline. The crazy hours and weekends he had put in had not gone unnoticed, and the praise lavished on his team at the grand opening of their client's luxury hotel earlier that week was all the acknowledgment Gabe needed to realize he had made the right choice in moving to this city. The fact that the money he was making could easily afford him a two-bedroom condo in the exclusive neighborhood of Meguro didn't hurt, either.

Yet, despite having relocated thousands of miles to the other side of the world, his mind would not let go of the bite of his past. Which was why, when faced with the prospect of his first free weekend and the boxes he had yet to unpack, he had looked up *Saron*'s location on the spur of the moment and decided to take a gamble.

He had promised himself this move would not be just a fresh start for his mind, but for his body, too. That he would start taking risks in his personal life again. That he would not let the bastard who had made it impossible for him to ever have a satisfying physical relationship win.

Fifteen minutes into his first drink and Gabe wondered whether he had made a bad choice. So far, Ethan, the bartender, had helped him field a burly, yakuza-looking type with tattoos up the side of his neck, three old men with sweaty palms and bald patches, and a couple of young guys who looked barely past the legal age of drinking.

With his lean build, dark hair, and blue eyes, Gabe knew he was an attractive prospect. Add in that he was a foreigner and he was coming to the conclusion that he had become a beeline for all the men in the bar who wanted to make a conquest out of the white guy – a white notch in the proverbial bedpost. They all wanted to fuck him or be fucked by him.

A cynical half-smile twisted his lips at that thought. If only they knew.

He raised a hand to the back of his neck and rubbed the warm spot that had been bothering him for a while. Something made him look up from his drink then – call it instinct or that subconscious voice that warns of imminent danger. Movement in the mirror opposite the bar caught his gaze. Or, more precisely, a lack of it.

Stormy gray eyes pierced him from the other end of the club. They locked on him, a beam of light in the gloom. Transfixing him. Immobilizing him.

Gabe's breath caught in his throat, every muscle in his body tightening in fight-or-flight mode.

The man sat apart from the crowd, alone at a table that could have accommodated three, a tumbler full of dark liquid clasped casually in his left hand. His red silk tie was crooked, as if he had slipped a finger through the knot to loosen it. The top two buttons on his white shirt were open, revealing tan skin covering toned muscles and a hint of curls.

Gabe couldn't tell whether his hair was dark brown or dirty blond. It was hard to say in the dim light. What wasn't hard to see were the subtle and not-so-subtle stares the other men in the bar were giving the stranger.

With his stubbled face, smoldering looks, and what appeared to be an incredibly ripped body beneath a custom-tailored charcoal suit, the man looked like a king sitting on a throne, commanding a roomful of servants. Servants who appeared more than willing to either get fucked by him or fuck him if he so much as lifted his little finger.

And a man like that would not have to ask twice.

Envy and irritation flashed through Gabe at that thought, shattering the spell he found himself under. He broke eye contact, shocked by the feelings suddenly flooding him, and glared at his half-empty glass. It seemed to mock him, as if it were a reflection of his own life. A half-empty, broken shell. Incapable of touching someone or to be touched.

Gabe lifted the glass and downed the rest of the drink with an angry flick of his wrist. Fire singed his throat. He welcomed the burning sensation, hoping it would calm the pounding in his chest and the tightness in his belly and groin that told him his body had reacted to the stranger.

A full glass of scotch appeared next to his empty tumbler.

Gabe looked up at Ethan, puzzled.

A remorseful grimace flashed across the bartender's face. "Looks like we're no longer the two hottest bastards in this joint. Here, compliments of the King."

Gabe stared at the drink before slowly looking over his shoulder, his pulse picking up speed.

Gray Eyes raised his glass in a toast. A teasing smile played on his sculptured lips before he knocked back his drink.

You're kidding me.

Gabe tried to block out the heated tingle running across his skin at the stranger's cocky smirk and the way his powerful throat muscles worked when he swallowed. He turned to Ethan.

"That's his *actual* name?"

Ethan grunted. "Well, no. But the asshole sure acts like one."

There was movement in the mirror opposite Gabe.

Read One Night today

AFTERWORD

To all my friends who helped make this possible. You know who you are.

To you, my readers. Thank you for reading Drake and Roman's story. I hope you loved this fifth book in the Twilight Falls series. I would be grateful if you could leave a review on Goodreads or on the store where you purchased this book. Reviews help readers like you find my books and I truly appreciate your honest opinions about my stories.

Make sure to sign up to my store newsletter for special deals on my books and new release alerts. Or you can sign up to my author newsletter instead to get upcoming release notifications, sneak peeks, and giveaways.

BOOKS BY A.M. SALINGER

NIGHTS

One Night - 1

The Escort - 2

Tokyo Heat - 3

Sweet Obsession - 4

Sweet Possession - 5

The Proposition - 6

Undisclosed - 7

Hush - 8

One Day - 9

TWILIGHT FALLS

Alex - 1

Carter - 2

Hunter - 3

Wyatt - 4

Drake - 5

Tristan - 6

Miles - 7

ABOUT THE AUTHOR

Ava Marie Salinger is the romance pen name of an Amazon bestselling author with a passion for writing addictive tales. Known for her action-packed and thrilling urban fantasy novels, she has expanded her repertoire with the introduction of the M/M urban fantasy romance series Fallen Messengers. Additionally, she has penned the scorching hot contemporary M/M romance series Nights and Twilight Falls as A.M. Salinger. When not immersed in her writing, Ava can be found curating inspiring music playlists, indulging in her love for nature, marveling at the latest gadgets, and savoring Chinese cuisine.

You can find all of Ava's books on her author store at
shop.adstarrling.com